PARISIAN GHOSTS 2

GHOSTS OF THE CRUSADE

JANNA RUTH

ISBN: 978-1-7386160-2-2 (eBook)

ISBN: 978-1-7386160-3-9 (Paperback)

Contents

A Note on Sensitive Topics

This is a book about ghosts, so naturally death plays a rather large part. If you don't like spoilers, and you're cool with everything, skip this note, and start the book. If you want to be prepared, read on. I'm writing this because reading should be fun, not a nasty surprise.

In this book, Alix struggles a lot as she comes to terms with the fact the man she loves is dead. Her grief is explored in depth and can be a little overwhelming at times. But don't worry, she'll pick herself up again.

Our heroine continues to be more curious and self-sacrificing than is good for her. For this book, that means less crawling through catacombs and more encounters with crazy ghosts, leading to a confrontation with guns, swords, and psychosis.

As expected in a ghost series, the nature of some characters' untimely deaths is revealed. Some scenes can be creepy or macabre, with graveyards and mausoleums making frequent appearances. There's also a sinister organisation that does not respect the sanctity of death, experimenting on corpses and skeletons alike, and willing to protect their work by any means necessary.

While not on scene, the exact nature of a child's death is revealed. Afterwards, Alix faces her fear of drowning through a vision and an actual drowning.

The series will be full of action with physical confrontations between the living and the dead, but our heroine is scrappy and will gain some strong supporters along the way.

Happy to tag along? Then join Alix in this new ghostly adventure on the streets of Paris!

Love, Janna

Grab your Free Copy

When an undead movie star asks you for a small favour, you know you're gonna be in deep trouble.

Seeing ghosts is just something I've learnt to live with. They're everywhere I go, especially since I chose to study history at the

Sorbonne, one of the oldest universities in the world. While on a class trip to the Pantheon, where France's great men—and women!—reside, I get introduced to the fabulous Josephine Baker! One of her war medals has gone missing, and she wants me to find its whereabouts.

Who could say no to a flapper girl turned movie star turned war hero? Little do I know agreeing to do so will send me on a wild-goose chase across the country with a ghostly pet cheetah, hidden walkways, and a murder attempt.

Follow Alix on her first big ghost adventure two years prior to the events of Parisian Ghosts.

Sign up to my Story Seeker mailing list and grab the prequel for free

CHAPTER 1

"You're a ghost."

I stare at Gaspar as if I'm seeing him for the first time. The floppy brown hair that falls into his eyes, the black-painted fingernails, the hoodie with some obscure band logo. I'm looking for the smile that always made my heart leap, but today it's missing. For a good reason.

Gaspar is dead. Has been dead from the moment I met him. That's just perfect. The first time I've found someone who likes me as much as I like them, someone who accepts all my quirks, and they're not even alive.

You need to spend more time with the living, they said. And here I am, my heart aching for a ghost.

The look in Gaspar's eyes is tortured. The longer I hold his gaze, the more he falls apart. Finally, he looks away and mumbles, "I'm sorry."

He's apologising for being *dead*.

"You don't... you..." I bite my tongue, trying to sort my words. But my mind swirls, picking up memories and remixing them, searching for clues. How could I have missed it? He never ate, never drank, never bloody answered his phone!

Love. That's the only explanation I have. I was in love, completely blind to all the little things that should have tipped me off. I feel stupid and betrayed, which is even more stupid because it's not like he did this on purpose: die in an accident so he could befriend and romance me.

I blink and look at the things left by friends and classmates, people who actually knew him. The flowers are long dead, while the letters have been soaked by the rain a dozen times over. He's been dead for three weeks.

"Did you know?" I whisper.

"Not at first."

My head whips around, my eyes find his again. "What do you mean?" I've never met anyone so early in the afterlife, so soon after their death. Emily came the closest, and she'd known about her death. Another thought interrupts the one I'm having. Gaspar totally saw Emily and kept quiet about it.

"I... it was confusing," he admits. "At first I had no idea. I didn't even remember riding my bike. Just staring at the scene of the accident in confusion. And then you appeared."

So at least he hadn't been lying from the start. "So, when did you know?"

"For sure?" Gaspar wrinkles his nose as he thinks about it, "After you told me you could see ghosts. I guess I was in denial until then."

Memories of that evening by the Seine float to the surface. His reaction devastated me. He broke my heart. I thought that he was angry at me for being so ridiculous, that I had somehow offended him. It didn't make much sense at the time, which made it even harder to deal with. He'd been nothing short of amazing and then bam, total rejection.

Now I get it. Up until then, interacting with me had served as an illusion of being alive for him. My confession had ripped the Band-Aid off. Without knowing it, I had confirmed his greatest fear.

"My flatmates and colleagues mourned me," Gaspar explains. "It was confusing because how could I be dead when I'd just gone out with you? When you touched me? Kissed me?"

I swallow the biggest lump. My cursed affliction had not only made me believe the man I'd fallen in love with was alive, it had also prevented Gaspar from adjusting to his new reality. "But you came back."

"Of course I came back!" He takes a step towards me and puts his hands on my elbows. "Alix, I acted like a dumbass. It's not your fault I got hit by the van. If anything, you made it so much... nicer, I guess. Without you, I would have been completely lost, but you made this transition easier. I'm dead, yes, but I'm still here. I can still do things. Be with someone."

Once again, I swallow. I'm still hugging myself, despite his fingers on my elbows, unwilling to go there. I kissed a ghost! Luckily only in private. I can't imagine how stupid I would have looked if I'd done it in public. Goose bumps are running down my spine.

But this isn't about me—at least not yet. In spite of myself, I've got a million questions about the transition from living to dead. I didn't know that ghosts could be so traumatised by their death that they would go in denial. It makes a lot of sense, though. After all, death is one of the most traumatic things that can happen to anyone. I can't even blame Gaspar for dealing with it on his own, and I wish I could have been there for him. If my abilities are good for anything, then surely it's this.

I push my own feelings into a dark corner of my mind and concentrate on Gaspar. After a quick glance around me to make sure no one is watching, I ask him, "Are you okay?"

"Am I okay?" Gaspar blinks. "I don't think that matters anymore, does it?"

"It matters to me." After all, I'm the ghost whisperer who helps out ghosts. That, and I do like him a lot. "I can't imagine how hard it must be to... well, to be dead, I suppose."

The corner of Gaspar's mouth twitches. "It's different than I expected. I mean nobody tells you about all this. I thought you'd just cease to exist and that'd be that."

I nod. "It's a lot, I suppose. There are whole communities of ghosts out there. My grandmother and her best friend even host parties."

"That's cool." Slowly, the smile I love so much returns to his face.

"Where are you staying?" I ask, curious as to where he'd go when he wasn't with me.

Gaspar lets go of me and scratches the back of his head before running his hand through his hair. All his little gestures cause me pain. He seems so alive when he really isn't.

"At first, I just went home. My flatmates ignored me, but I didn't know where else to go. I left when things got worse."

"Worse?"

"When they talked about me while I was standing there, shouting at them that I was still alive. That I was standing right next to them. That I couldn't be dead because I'd met this amazing girl. And then my room was cleared out."

I swallow hard. "I'm so sorry."

"Not your fault." He gives me a heartbreaking little shrug. "Since then, I've pretty much just wandered the streets of Paris, always coming back here. Which is stupid, because why would I want to come back here?"

It's one question I can answer for him. "Because this is where people remember you." I sidestep him and squat down to pick up a photo of Gaspar. The sturdy cardboard has withstood the weather a little better than the letters. In the picture, Gaspar is a few years younger. His hair is shorter, but his nails are already black. He's fooling around in front of the poster of a festival line-up, tongue out, eyes wide open, and index finger and little fingers extended.

"This was at Lollapalooza a few years back. I went there with my friend from school, Gustave," Gaspar explains. "He studies Sociology with me."

"I think I met him."

"Did you?"

"Does he wear the same kind of band shirts as you do?" When Gaspar nods, I sigh. "I thought so. I asked him about you and he..." I stop when I hear footsteps and chatter behind me.

For a few heartbeats, I don't move, straining my ears instead of looking. Fortunately, with the picture in my hand, I don't look strange to anyone. Just another mourner. I could probably go on talking, but I don't.

A couple of young women walk past behind me, their heels clicking on the tarmac. When they're gone, I release my breath and turn to Gaspar. "You can't stay here."

"Agreed. This place is depressing. Except..." his eyes wander to the opposite side, "where I met you."

I shake off the memory of our first macabre but beautiful en-counter. "Where would you like to stay?"

"With you."

He's so attached to me, and that's my fault. I'm the ghost whisperer. I should have known better. But nobody teaches you that stuff.

I wonder if the policeman I'd met would teach me or if he's as lost as I am. I tell Gaspar, "You can't stay at my place." Odile would have a field day if she heard me talking to myself. Besides, it would be too much, even for me.

Flustered, Gaspar gasps. "Oh, I didn't mean to suggest that. I agree. We're definitely not at that point in our relationship."

Trying not to flinch, I nod hastily. "Agreed."

"I just meant that I'd like to stay close to you," Gaspar explains, a hint of desperation in his voice. "I'm new to all of this and I don't know who else to turn to, but more importantly, I really enjoy spending time with you. It sucks that I only met you after the accident."

Oh yeah, it sucks a lot.

"I know you probably don't want me around anymore, but..."

I shoot up and whirl around. "That's not true." A group of students on the other side cast pitiful glances at me. I'm tempted to shout just like Gaspar did, that I'm not some crazy mourner in denial. That he's right here. But he isn't. Not in any form that matters to people. And it hurts.

When they're gone, I keep my voice low. "I know a place where you can stay."

"No." For the first time ever, Victor Hugo has the stairs to the crypt blocked for me by the military ghosts who run the day-to-day operations on the upper level.

After some thought, I took Gaspar to the Panthéon. Philippe was happy for me to take over his shift. He never asks a lot of questions, which I appreciate. He probably finds it strange how invested I am in our work, but since he benefits from it, he doesn't care too much about the why.

So far so good, but on the way down we are refused entry. "No what?"

"No foreign ghosts allowed."

That's right. For some reason, the Panthéon ghosts are incredibly protective of their prestigious resting place. They allow ghosts up in the foyer but not down here.

I point to Gaspar. "This is Gaspar."

Immediately, Victor's face softens. "Oh, kid." The pity in his voice is almost too much to bear.

Gaspar looks at me in confusion but wisely keeps his mouth shut.

"You went back to the catacombs, didn't you?" Victor asks.

It takes me a moment to realise what he means. "Oh, no. I mean, yes, I did, but Gaspar's always been... like that. I just didn't notice."

If I thought the pity was unbearable before, now it almost suffocates me. Victor looks as if he wants to give me a hug, but I know I can't take it. Not here, not from a ghost right now.

"I'm sorry," Gaspar whispers.

I take a deep breath and continue with the plan. "Yes, I know, it's all very tragic. At least now I can introduce you. Victor, this is Gaspar. Gaspar, this is Victor Hugo."

It's not entirely new to Gaspar that I'm hanging out with all the famous ghosts of Paris, but his eyes widen nonetheless. "*The* Victor Hugo? Oh, wow. It's an honour, sir." Gaspar takes a step forward and holds out his hand.

Victor clears his throat, stopping him in his tracks. As usual, admiration softens him, though. "The pleasure is mine, though I'm confident this is not the outcome we all wanted."

"No," Gaspar admits, his face darkening again.

"He needs a place to stay." Carefully, I pick up the threads of our earlier conversation. "I thought..."

Victor sighs heavily. "I'm sorry, Alix, but I'm afraid that's not possible. The good news, though, is that as a ghost, he doesn't need a home. He can stay wherever he wants."

"But not here?"

"Not here." Victor remains adamant. Behind the barrier of military ghosts, the other crypt dwellers are watching us. They leave it to Victor, but I can tell from their expressions that they won't come to my aid.

"Why not?" I'm getting a little frustrated. My eyes are burning, which tells me how thin this layer of productivity is that protects me from the feelings lurking under my skin.

Victor still looks so damn sympathetic. "This place is reserved for the great men—and women—of France. What has Gaspar ever done for France?"

That's it? A bloody ivory tower? I feel the anger rising inside me. "Well, unfortunately he never had the chance to be great. He didn't live to be eighty-three. Would you have been one of the greats if you'd died at twenty-two?" None of the people here died young. They all had time to hone their craft and do great things.

"Look," Gaspar says quietly, "I don't think I would've ever achieved anything remarkable."

Oh no, he's not going to self-reject now. I'm seething with anger as I snap at him, "You don't know that."

"Alix..." Victor says quietly. "You're upset."

"Of course I'm upset! You call yourselves the great figures of France but you won't help a new ghost. After all I've done for you. Will you also deny me when it's my time?" I never thought my time with Victor and the others was limited until now.

Victor stares at his feet, uncharacteristically meek.

"Wow..."

My mocking tone brings his face back up. "I have no doubt that you will do great things and earn your place here."

As if. I have no such illusions about myself. You have to be truly exceptional to be inducted into the Panthéon. And being a history student won't get me there.

Rousseau approaches and whispers in Victor's ear. Victor pulls a face, but after a moment he gives in. "Very well. Gaspar can stay. For a little while." Immediately, the military ghosts return to their posts upstairs.

I give Rousseau a grateful look, glad that at least one of my ghosts hasn't forgotten his humble beginnings.

"He probably won't be able to hold onto the room for long, though." Victor looks at Gaspar. "Do you have any special connection with the Panthéon, young man?"

Gaspar rubs the back of his head. "Not really. I've only visited once, ages ago."

I take Gaspar's hand and squeeze his fingers. "He's got me." Then I pull something out of my bag. "And this."

It's the picture Gustave left behind. Part of me feels bad that I've taken something so personal and meaningful, but it's exactly what's needed to make sure Gaspar has a strong hold on this place.

"You may hide it behind my tomb," Victor offers kindly. He takes a step aside, finally letting me and Gaspar pass.

I feel all eyes on me as I descend into the crypt, pulling Gaspar with me. He looks around in amazement, his mouth opening and closing frequently. We reach the writers' alcove and I let go of him to place the picture of him in a crevice behind Victor's tomb.

"It's not the same as being buried here, but it comes close. Josephine Baker's bones aren't here either, and yet she has a real hold on this place."

Gaspar huffs in amusement. "I still can't believe you're friends with all those people we learned about in history books."

I smile at him. "Well, now you'll be friends too. I hope." I'll be very angry with Victor and the others if they're going to shun Gaspar despite this arrangement.

"We'll see about that," Gaspar says. "I can still leave, can't I?"

"Of course. You're not restricted by anything. Not while I'm still here." There is no way I will ever forget Gaspar as long as I live.

He takes my hands in his. "So, what happens now?"

"Well, I'll leave you to acclimatise to your new surroundings while I go home. I work on Tuesdays, Wednesdays, and Sundays. Beyond that, I'll be at the Sorbonne if you need anything." It may be a bit abrupt, but I need some space right now. To breathe and to think. And to feel.

Fortunately, Gaspar doesn't protest. "Thanks for everything you do."

As he leans in, I stumble backwards and let go of his hands. "I have to go."

I practically flee the crypt.

Chapter 2

After leaving Gaspar with Victor, I go straight to Gaby's apartment. She's still at work when I arrive, but a neighbour lets me into the stairwell so I can wait outside her flat. I feel numb as I sit at the top of the stairs, trying my best to keep my spiralling thoughts at bay.

For three weeks, I've been hanging out with a ghost.

I kissed a ghost.

My boyfriend is a ghost.

Gaspar is dead.

What was I thinking?

I breathe through my teeth and press the palms of my hands into my eyes to keep the tears from spilling over. Why do these things keep happening to me? No! Not this way. Not...

"Alix?" Gaby's voice sounds from below me. She's balancing a bag of produce on her hip and looking up at me with a worried expression. "Have you heard from Gaspar?"

Instead of answering, I let out the most pathetic half-choked sob.

Gaby runs up the stairs, drops her shopping bag, and throws her arms around me. "Oh, darling! What is it? Is he...?"

And then I remember. The worry of the last two days has been swept aside by the terrible revelation I have just had. Before I found out that Gaspar was a ghost, I thought he'd been shot in the catacombs. We were being pursued by le Chevalier d'Os and one of his henchmen, a woman who must have been a ghost whisperer like me, because she'd seen Gaspar. It worked to our advantage as Gaspar managed to draw her away from me.

"It's not..." I choke out, trying to comfort Gaby only to realise that it doesn't matter if he's been shot or not. He's still... "Dead."

Gaby's embrace tightens as she pulls my head into her chest. "No!"

"Yes." And suddenly the dam breaks. I can't hold back the tears a minute longer. It's like the Seine is pouring out of my eyes. I don't stand a chance as I shake and tremble, sobbing my broken little heart out.

Somehow, Gaby manages to manoeuvre me into her flat, where I collapse on the floor, still unable to string a proper sentence together and explain the important difference between Gaspar having been dead all this time and just dying. There really isn't any. The former is just laced with my own embarrassment at having fallen for a dead man in the first place.

What will Gaby think of me? She's always been supportive of me—at least after that first little hiccup—but this is too much, too out there even for me. She'll think I've really lost it. Or worse. That I'm delusional. Am I delusional? I guess that depends on what I'm going to do next.

But first I have to calm down. It takes me most of the next half hour to dry my tears and gather enough breath to tell her the whole story. It's like pulling teeth, but if I can't tell Gaby, then I can't tell anyone.

Sniffling, I straighten my back. "He's a ghost."

Gaby frowns at me. "Is that a good thing? Is that how you found out?"

I shake my head. "No, I didn't." My voice shakes at the admission. "What I mean is..." I have to take another deep breath. "Do you remember the student who died?"

I'd been so preoccupied with the catacombs ghosts, Emily's request, and meeting Gaspar that I hadn't paid much attention to the campus tragedy. I hadn't even bothered to learn his name. What a fine ghost whisperer I am.

"You mean the cyclist who was hit by a van?"

"That's him."

Gaby's face falls. She stares at me for a few uncomfortable heart-beats. Then she pulls out her phone and checks something on it. Finally, she mumbles, "Gaspar du Charbonneau." It's on the bloody Internet.

She looks up again. "This is your Gaspar? You..." Gaby doesn't even have words for it.

Neither do I. I nod, hiccuping as I do so. My eyes start to burn again as shame and grief overtake me. "It's him."

"Did you...?"

I shake my head.

"So, all this time...?"

"He was dead." With another shaky breath, I regain some composure. "I never met the real Gaspar. He was always a ghost. I just didn't notice." Silly me. I really *do* spend too much time with the dead.

"Oh, Alix!" Gaby pulls me back into her arms. "I'm so sorry. Why didn't he say anything?" She sounds angry.

But Gaspar doesn't deserve her anger. This is on me. "He was in denial. Apparently, his mind went into shock. And since I interacted with him, he never dared to go there. Until I told him of my ability. That's why he reacted so badly. He didn't think I was crazy. He didn't want to admit that he was really dead."

Gaby pulls me closer and strokes my hair. "Don't you dare blame yourself. Oh, ma puce. I'm so sorry this happened to you."

I let out a mocking snort. "Who else would it happen to?" Somehow I doubt Officer Roubert would fall in love with a ghost without noticing. Speaking of him… "Remember the policeman?"

"What about him?" Gabby lets go of me and knits her eyebrows. "Did he tell you?"

"Sort of. But that's not it. Apparently, he's like me. A ghost whisperer."

Gaby's eyes widen. "No way! He's a ghost whisperer?"

I nod, welcoming the change of subject. "Yes. And he wants to talk to me." I went to the catacombs to find other ghost whisperers, and despite my utter failure down there, I managed to stumble across one at least. "Do you think I should hear him out?" Not that I'll have a choice. He made it very clear that he had more questions. If anything, he just gave me some time to come to terms with my dead boyfriend.

"Yes, I think that's a good idea. He might know some tips and tricks."

"Like how to tell the living from the dead?" I say with enough bitterness to make me cringe.

Gaby gives me a pitiful look. "Maybe." She shrugs. "I'm just saying you should give him a chance. He seems pretty nice for a policeman. And it sounds like he wants to help you."

"Yeah." My interest in the subject fades and my thoughts return to Gaspar. "What should I do now?"

"About?"

I whisper his name, "Gaspar."

Gaby winces. "Well, I don't know. Has he contacted you again?" I can see how strange this is for her now that she knows he doesn't really exist.

"Yes. I found him at the scene of the accident. They still have flowers for him there. We talked and I put him up at the Panthéon for the time being."

"You introduced him to Victor?"

"It didn't go very well, but Victor agreed to let him stay there for now." I see Gaby chewing on something. "What?"

She sighs. "I'm sorry." This doesn't bode well. "It's just... well, you can't really go on now that you know, can you?"

It's the question of the day. If you would've asked me a month ago if I'd ever consider a relationship with a ghost, I'd have been horrified. But now I'm already in one. "I really like him."

"I know."

"He's a good guy. Funny, kind, supportive."

"Dead."

I swallow hard. "If we'd been together before he died, would you be asking me the same question?"

Gaby blinks and takes a deep breath. Not good. "Yes."

A groan escapes my throat. This isn't fair. I finally meet the perfect guy for me—after he dies.

Gaby shuffles closer and takes me in her arms again. "I'm sorry. You don't have to think about it right now. You only just found out. It's okay to hold on to him a little longer." She kisses my hair.

That's all I get. A little longer with Gaspar, while he finds his footing in the afterlife. And then I'm expected to move on, even though he's right there with his smile and his kiss. I can touch him and he can touch me, but for everyone else he's not real. I might as well have imagined him. Like a proper basket case.

While Gaby strokes my hair and rocks me gently back and forth like a baby, I tear myself apart mercilessly, dragging out all my faults and failures. It's not socially acceptable to be with a ghost. Heck, it's not even socially acceptable to believe in ghosts. And yet here I am, desperately wanting a man I can't have a future with. Not in this life.

CHAPTER 3

It's a strange situation. Gaby told me to mourn Gaspar, but how do you mourn someone who's still here? Every time I go to work, he greets me with a beaming smile and tells me all about the famous residents I used to look after alone. Despite their initial reluctance, they seem to have accepted Gaspar into their fold. Not as an equal but more like an adorable puppy. He's not one of them, but they don't mind and let him run his course.

Meanwhile, I go back and forth with my decision to stay with him. My head says no, but my heart can't let him go.

I have, however, taken an interest in Gaspar's real life. I stalked his social media profiles—swallowing hard at the memorial page set up on Facebook—and those he'd been friends with. Among them his coworker Marie at *Chambelland*. At last I know why she always looked so sad. Now I just have to work up the courage to talk to her about him.

Since my first visit, I've become a regular at the little café, getting my usual order of a pain au chocolat and a coffee. Marie smiles at me as I order and goes through her usual routine of asking me how I am.

The correct answer would be a big fucking mess. But to explain that I would have to tell her about my ability to see ghosts, and I don't think that would go down too well with her. Instead, I give the socially acceptable answer of, "Ça va bien," and ask her how she is. "Really?"

Marie's smile stutters. "Fine... I mean..."

I put my hand on hers as she hands me my coffee. "If you need to talk, I'm a good listener." I nod my head towards a small table nearby where I intend to sit. Normally, I would just leave immediately, letting her know I mean it.

It takes ten minutes for the café to quiet down. I finish my food and drink but stay around a little longer until Marie finally finds some time to slip away from the counter.

With her eyes on the door, she sinks into the chair, not that it's a very soft one. All the chairs in *Chambelland* are Art Nouveau, filigree wrought-iron chairs. Pretty and delicate but not comfortable.

"You come here quite often," Marie begins.

"It was a recommendation." From a dead man. "I'm Alix, by the way. I study history at Sorbonne."

Marie's eyes light up, if only for a few seconds. "Marie. Law."

"Wow. You must be pretty smart."

She rolls her eyes. "A lot of memorising, mostly. So... what did you want to talk about?"

The ball lands in my lap and for a moment I'm too scared to speak. I have to remind myself that I need this. I need to talk to someone who actually knew Gaspar, and I don't feel comfortable finding his other friend again.

"I knew Gaspar," I whisper.

Her whole attitude changes. Before, Marie had been reserved and unsure. Now her eyes are wide and she leans forward. "You did?" Tears form at the corners of her eyes. "I can't get over it. One day he messes around with me, tricks me into taking his shift—again!—and then... and then..." Her voice trails off. "I was angry at him!"

"Angry?"

"Because he let me down. At the handover. He never came." Marie takes a shaky breath. "And then our manager called and said she was on her way. That I should close the café." Tears are now streaming down her face. "I was angry, and he was dead."

I move my chair around the table to put an arm around her shoulders. "You didn't do anything wrong. I'm so sorry."

Marie takes a moment to recover. When she does, she dabs her eyes and asks, "So, how did you know him?"

How can I lie to Marie when she has just bared her soul to me? And yet I don't want her to think I'm taking her for a ride. In the end, I try to stick to the facts as much as possible. "Gaspar and I met at university and we... I guess we hit it off. He took me to a party down in the catacombs, and..." I blink hard.

How happy I'd been. I can still feel the butterflies dancing in my stomach. Even though he was dead, Gaspar made me feel alive. He challenged me to try bold new things and introduced me to a whole new world. Beyond ghosts and death, although in the end that's all I found there.

"You guys were dating?" There is still some reserve in her voice. She probably didn't just work with Gaspar but was friends with him. And of course, he never told her about me.

"One date," I whisper.

"I'm sorry." The reluctance finally melts away. "He really liked the catacombs. I was never brave enough to go with him. They're dangerous, you know, but I guess so is cycling to school." Marie dabs at her eyes again. "I think Gaspar was right. What's life without a little adventure from time to time?"

I like that about him. He never hesitated when I asked him to venture deeper into the catacombs. And while we both got more adventure than we signed up for, it was also exhilarating. Too bad the catacombs have been taken over by some madmen.

The door opens, and a customer enters. Marie almost jumps out of her chair. "Bonjour!" She gives me a longing look as she hurries back behind the counter.

I watch as she slaps on a fake smile and serves the customer but there are more on their way in and it doesn't look like we'll get another break soon. So, instead, I write down my number on a napkin and slide it over the counter. "I'll be back tomorrow."

The smile she gives me may be fleeting, but it's real. I feel a kind of kinship between us—two people mourning the same person. It makes me feel a little less alone.

Outside my ghost sphere, the world just goes on. I spend time with my family, go out with Gaby, and attend my classes. Madame Canet's class still revolves around the catacombs. I wish we could move on, but unfortunately, I don't have any say in the curriculum.

However, I do seem to have an influence on today's lecture as Madame Canet brought out my homework to share with the class. It got top marks, but I'm not sure it needs to be dissected by the class.

The assignment was to summarise the situation in the late-18th century and the factors that led to the decision of the Quarry Inspection Department, before critically examining the actions taken and discussing how it could've been done better. Of course, I've written a lengthy rebuttal to the action taken, advocating for the dead.

"Alix made some interesting points in her essay." Madame Canet has put a few quotes of mine on the screen. The slide is entitled 'The Dignity of Death'.

My own words are staring back at me: *The most atrocious act was to treat the remains of the deceased as nothing more than building material. The bones lost all meaning and purpose when they were rearranged and removed from their resting place. It would have been kinder to burn the remains and scatter the ashes to the wind.*

Naturally, Théo's hand immediately shoots up. "What difference does it make?" he asks. "Either way, the remains would have been moved and dislocated."

Madame Canet looks at me now to answer him because it's all there in my essay. "The difference is that one would have been an economic choice that solved the problem, while the other would have led to a grotesque display for tourists to feast on."

"But it wasn't open to tourists for almost a hundred years," Théo argues. "It was to the public in 1874, so you can't really blame the 18th-century people for the sensationalism of later generations."

He's got a point there. "So, you agree that the catacombs shouldn't be open to the public? That it's pure sensationalism that excites people?"

Théo laughs, incredulous that I would try to trap him. "Au contraire! That was the end of the 19th century. It was all about the grotesque. Nowadays, however, it's all about preserving history.

You could argue that there is a deeper appreciation of the dead than ever before."

"You think the majority of people who visit the catacombs today think of the six million dead in the same way as they would at a Holocaust memorial?" It's not an ideal comparison, since each of the six million ghosts in the catacombs died of an individual cause, many of them quite naturally, rather than being systematically murdered, but it's an ossuary of similar proportions.

There's no laughter this time. Théo actually takes a moment to think about it, and I almost get my hopes up that he's finally understood the severity of death. But when he opens his mouth again, he shakes his head. "Not like that, no. But you can't really expect people to."

"Why not?" I ask him.

"Because they can't relate to any of the dead," Théo shoots back.

I'm well aware that the whole class is watching our exchange. Madame Canet seems delighted, while Gaby is chewing her lip nervously.

"With the Holocaust, there are still people who are related to the victims, and we all learnt about it at school. It's still very relevant," Théo explains. "With the catacombs, it's just a random graveyard under the ground."

Which brings us back to the 19th century. "So, it's all novelty, after all?"

Disgruntled, Théo glares at me. He crosses his arms. "Fine. There's a novelty aspect to it. But I don't think it's a bad thing."

I narrow my eyes. "How is that not bad?"

"Because it still serves as a reminder of how our city evolved. It's not about remembering someone buried there or reflecting on a momentous event. It's about showing the challenges that Paris had to face, and also how old our city is. How many people lived here before us." Satisfied that he's back on track, Théo nods.

His argument is good. I'm sure he got just as good a mark for his essay, even though he's arguing a completely different point of view. And yet, it frustrates me, because the fact remains that the ghosts in the catacombs are suffering. While we indulge our sensationalism and revel in the dark side of history, they suffer a terrible existence. If only I knew how to make Théo—or anyone else—see this.

There's really only one angle, and it's the one Madame Canet so aptly titled my slide with. "What about the dignity of the dead?"

Next to me, Gaby moans softly. I try not to let it get to me, I know she's just worried about me. Maybe now more than ever.

Théo looks uncomfortable. "Is that really history? I'm just saying. At what point do we slip into ethics?"

"Don't you think we should consider ethics when we study history?" We do it all the time when we look at historical events through our modern lenses. There's even a seminar we all took in year two.

Théo looks at Madame Canet, practically begging her to stop me. When she doesn't, he throws in the towel himself. "Fine, have it your way. If we were faced with the same decision today, I doubt very much that we'd come to the same conclusion. There would be no catacombs. But..." He just can't let it go. "The decision was made two-hundred-and-fifty years ago, so deal with it."

Deal with it. My eyes burn with frustration. What's the point of studying history if not to learn from it? If not to right our wrongs? I suppose that's not the standard reason for entering our field, though. And I have to admit, it wasn't mine either. Somewhere along the line it went from curiosity and interest to purpose. But my motivation is impossible for anyone to understand. To create a better future, sure. Creating one for those long dead? Not happening.

As Madame Canet moves the discussion forward, inviting other points of view, I dig my nails into my palms to keep from screaming. It reminds me of Gaspar. *They're still here,* I want to scream. But no one can see them.

Not even Gaby, who wouldn't dare argue with me. She puts her hand on my arm and whispers, "Let it go, Alix. Remember, you can't help all the ghosts." There is an undercurrent of "Look where it got you with Emily" in her words, and it only makes me abuse my hands more.

I need someone in my corner who really understands. Someone who's like me. A ghost whisperer.

It's time to give Officer Roubert a call.

CHAPTER 4

Officer Roubert agrees to meet me two days later in a fancy restaurant in the Marais—his choice, not mine. As he's promised to pay, I don't mind. It's better than meeting him at the police station. At least this is neutral ground.

When I arrive at the address, Roubert is already there with a cappuccino in front of him. It's about an hour before the lunch rush, so the restaurant is almost empty. Unlike the last time I saw him, Roubert is wearing a light shirt and beige trousers. He rises from his chair and we greet each other with a kiss on the cheek before he offers me the chair opposite.

"Would you like to order some wine?" he asks, handing me the menu.

"Will I need it?" I joke dryly.

Roubert smiles wanly. "Who knows? I prefer white."

"White it is then." At this rate, this is going to be one of those fancy business lunches that my older sister enjoys so much. I spend a few minutes studying the menu before deciding on the soup of the day and a salad.

"You aren't hungry?"

I haven't been hungry since I found out my boyfriend was a ghost. "Not really." Besides, even if he's the one paying, the prices are stomach-churning.

He waits until the waiter has left before he studies me as carefully as I studied the menu. His blue-eyed gaze betrays intelligence and a certain interest. It's disconcerting.

"Do I have something stuck in my teeth?" I ask, unable to hold his gaze for long.

"So, you're a ghost whisperer," he says, instead of answering my question.

At least I didn't have to bring it up. "I suppose so. What about you?"

"I can see them, too."

"And talk to them? Touch them?" I have to be careful what I say, or I might start crying again.

"All that."

He's really like me. "How...? How do you cope with it?" Blame it on my fragile mental state at the moment, but I'm desperate for any kind of help. Even from this stranger.

"Cope?" Roubert raises an eyebrow. Then he leans back and thinks. "I suppose I had a lot of guidance from my father. He's one of us too."

"Jealous!" My family put me in therapy because of the ghosts and will probably do it again when they hear about Gaspar.

Roubert chuckles. "I guess that makes things a lot easier."

I take a deep breath and wait for the waiter to pour our drinks. "So, you've never had to wonder you might not be all right in your head?"

"Not because of the ghosts," he jokes before quickly sobering up. "I'm sorry your experience wasn't like that."

I shrug and pick up my wine. Swirling it thoughtfully, I mutter, "I bet you never fell for a ghost either."

Roubert's face softens. "No, I can't say that I have."

Blinking hard, I take a good sip of my wine and force a smile. "So, you work for the police?"

"GoPol." Roubert hesitates a moment before shrugging. "The ghost police."

"What?" The question bursts out before I can stop myself. "You're joking."

He doesn't smile. "Not at all. It's a subdivision of Interpol, not exactly common knowledge. Most of my colleagues are ghost whisperers like you and me."

My jaw drops. For a few moments I just stare at him. It takes me a lot of effort to regain my composure. "What do you do? Solve ghost crimes?"

This time he can't help but laugh. "No. We usually leave that to the ghosts themselves. It's mostly intelligence work. I can't give you too many details, but we use ghosts to gather information."

"That's actually quite clever." Since ghosts are invisible to most people and can pass through walls, they'd make perfect spies. "How do you get them to cooperate? Just ask nicely?"

"Sometimes. Every ghost whisperer usually has a few close relationships. Of course, not every ghost makes a good spy. Most are too flaky. They forget what they were supposed to do or show up at the wrong time because time no longer matters to them, but they can be trained to a certain extent."

Training ghosts sounds a bit like treating them like pets, but I'm too fascinated by this purposeful cooperation to question it too much. "Do the ghosts get anything out of it?"

Roubert shrugs. "Not much as far as I can see, but most of them do it for two reasons. Group A is perpetually bored. They are more willing to do the tough jobs but hard to keep interested. You might find yourself abandoned. The second group does it out of a deep longing for meaning. I suppose it's their way of holding on to life. There are a lot of ex-police among them."

As if the police were the only ones with a purpose in life. "How do you keep ghosts from spying on you instead?"

"That's another aspect of our work. Finding potential leaks. A ghost on its own can't hurt us. But if they report to a ghost whisperer, that's a different problem altogether."

A shiver runs down my spine. "Is that why you wanted to talk to me?"

"Do you run a spy agency?" Roubert asks me bluntly.

"No! I'm just a student and part-time tourist guide."

He smiles suddenly and I realise he's just teasing me. "Then no, that's not why I wanted to talk to you."

I relax a little. The last thing I need right now is to be investigated by the police. Roubert seems nice enough, but thanks to my sister's fiancé, I have a healthy distrust of the police. "Then why did you?"

Our food arrives and for a moment we both focus on eating. Finally, Roubert replies, "We need to talk about what you saw down in the catacombs."

I swallow hard. Fortunately, the soup is so smooth that it just runs down my throat. "Do we have to?"

"Unfortunately, yes." He reaches across the table to help himself to some bread from the basket. "That's another aspect of my job. Keeping people from messing with the ghosts."

"What do you think they do down there?"

"You tell me." His blue eyes scrutinise me once more. "What exactly have you stumbled upon?"

I'd been too worried about Gaspar's fate to tell him about Emily. Unwilling to recount the gruesome details, I open the photo app on my phone and slide it across the table before I can lose my appetite.

Roubert has no such qualms. It probably comes with the job, but he continues to eat as he scrolls through the pictures on my phone. Finally, he taps the phone a few times. "Do you mind if I send them to my work email?"

"Not at all." After all, I promised Emily that I would bring her case to the attention of the police.

While he does his thing, I finish my soup. Though it's more a routine task; it became completely tasteless a few minutes ago.

"Who was she?" Roubert asks in a subdued voice.

"Her name was Emily Durant, she was a cataphile and a tour guide. Unofficially, of course. She stumbled upon this place called Ossa Arida and was killed for it."

"Do you know who killed her?" He's stopped eating, completely absorbed in the case.

I look around as if expecting the Chevalier to come out of the kitchen. "Emily said she was killed by someone called le Chevalier d'Os. He and a woman were the ones who shot at me and Gas—… just me."

Roubert nods thoughtfully. "I've heard of the Chevalier."

"He hangs out at the Crossroad of the Dead, if that helps." I would feel a lot better knowing that psycho was behind bars.

"I know. So far, his record is squeaky clean. All we have is rumour and hearsay."

"Ghost witnesses don't count?"

He winces. "Unfortunately not. We're still bound by mundane laws and courts." Roubert's gaze has hardened, his eyebrows drawn deep. "There is only one thing we can do. One thing we must do. Return to Ossa Arida."

The blood drains from my face. "No."

"Please. I need your help to find the place. It'll be safe with me."

I doubt very much that any place in the catacombs is safe. Certainly not the site of a murder.

As I shake my head, Roubert turns to pleading. "Please, Mademoiselle Dubois. You want us to catch him, don't you?"

"Ugh, only if you call me Alix." What am I doing here? I have a very good reason for staying out of this. I'm a civilian, for ghost's sake. I certainly don't owe it to Emily, who lied and manipulated me from the very beginning. But Roubert will be lost without my guidance, and I really *do* want the Chevalier caught and put behind bars.

Roubert smiles. "Alix, then. And if you have any questions or concerns—"

He's interrupted by a wild bang on the window. Roubert looks slightly irritated at the two people I know very well. Outside, my older sister Hélène and her fiancé Cédric are waving at me. Much to my chagrin, they decide to come in, smiling broadly.

"Alix!" My sister leans in and kisses me left and right. "Is that Gaspar?" she asks excitedly, taking in Roubert.

Before I can explain who he is, Cédric laughs. "Oh no. You haven't met Séb yet. Hélène, this is my cousin Sébastien. Séb, this is my fiancée Hélène."

I stare at Officer Roubert in shock. "You're cousins?"

Roubert looks a bit annoyed, and I get the impression he's not Cédric's biggest fan. That makes two of us. "I had no idea." He's obviously referring to our surprising connection, not his relationship with Cédric, although it could be both.

"How do you know Séb?" Cédric asks me as we exchange kisses, oblivious to the change in mood.

I squirm in my chair, not sure how to answer. Hélène knows about the ghosts, but she thinks they're all in my head, while Cédric is the last person I want to involve in any of this. My searching gaze finds Roubert—or I suppose it's Sébastien now.

He folds his napkin and leans back in his chair, as if to challenge Cédric. "Alix and I have official GoPol business to discuss. I'm afraid I can't divulge any details."

Cédric pulls up a chair for Hélène and then another for himself. "You're recruiting her, aren't you? Well, I want you to know that I found her first."

Hélène gives me a confused look. I'm glad she thinks her future husband is behaving strangely for once. "What do you mean, you found her first?" she asks Cédric.

Since I'm not a thing to be found, I appreciate her question.

Cédric puts his arm around her. "When you told me about Alix and her ghosts, I thought she'd be a perfect fit for GoPol. They're the ghost police."

He might as well have shouted it out loud for all to hear. Sébastien scowls at his cousin, while Hélène looks incredulous. "Say what?"

"The ghost police," Cédric doubles down. "Alix would be perfect for that. My cousin sees ghosts too. I can tell her, can't I?" he asks, far too late. "We're getting married soon."

Sébastien's face darkens even more. "Looks like you've already taken it upon yourself."

A sudden thought hits me. "Wait! Did you arrange this for me?"

"No," Sébastien says quickly. "And for the record, I am not trying to recruit you. It doesn't work that way."

"Then how does it work?" Cédric asks in a pseudo-investigative tone.

"Can you all stop for a moment?" Hélène looks terribly pale. "Is this for real? Or is this an elaborate prank by you and Alix?"

I'm offended that she even thinks I'm in cahoots with Cédric. Anything so she doesn't have to believe me.

Cédric takes her hand. "It's true, darling. I'm sorry I didn't tell you right away, but you seemed upset and... well..." He nods towards his cousin. "I wasn't sure how much I could tell you."

"You didn't seem to have any qualms about it just now," Sébastien mutters. If I'm not mistaken, there isn't much love lost between these two cousins. "Anyway." He stands up, his chair scraping across the floor. "I'll email you the details later," he tells me. "Don't worry about the bill. I'll take care of that." With a final nod to Cédric and Hélène, he heads for the bar to pay for our lunch.

"He's a strange one," Hélène comments as he leaves the restaurant.

Personally, I like Sébastien a lot better than his cousin, but I know better than to get involved in other people's family drama.

"Always been a bit of a loner. Very dedicated to his work," Cédric tells us, once again revealing personal details about Sébastien without a second thought.

"It comes with the talent," I whisper. If it weren't for Gaby, I'd be all alone too.

Hélène sighs. "Talent, huh? I can't believe ghosts really exist."

She owes me a major apology, but I don't want to force it. The dead will rise before my big sister admits she was wrong.

"They do." Cédric, of all people, takes my side, suddenly my staunchest advocate. "Not that I've ever met one, but you can't grow up with the Rouberts and not believe. I'd always hoped to meet one, but it wasn't to be."

Hélène looks at him as if he'd grown two heads. And yet, now it's *him* saying it, she doesn't argue. "I think I need a moment to wrap my head around all this."

"I have to go," I announce, eager to get out of this strange situation.

"We'll drive you home," Cédric offers.

"I've got my bike."

"It fits on the back. I recently got a new carrier."

How do I get rid of them? Apparently not at all, because Hélène puts her hands on mine and begs me with her eyes. "Please, Alix, let us take you home. You don't look too good."

Gee, I wonder why that is.

"Fine. Whatever."

Chapter 5

The drive home is exactly as bad as I thought it would be. I'm in the back seat with Cédric driving, and Hélène sits next to him. As expected, driving in Paris is pure madness. I'd have got home much quicker on my bike.

"So how did you meet Cédric's cousin?" Hélène asks, looking straight ahead.

I roll my eyes. "I didn't know he was his cousin." I wouldn't have come if I had known, though that's not fair to Sébastien. He seems fine.

She gives me a strange look. "Am I not going to get an answer?"

"Do you want an answer?"

Hélène's shoulders hunch. "Is it ghosts?"

"Yeah." Not exactly, but it might as well be.

She swallows before smiling at me. "It's okay. You can tell me now."

"Can I now?" Where was this supportive sister before a policeman told her that ghosts were real? But very well, if Hélène thinks she can handle it, she'll get her answer. "I met Sébastien in the catacombs when I was there on ghost business. The ghost I was following turned out to have been murdered, and it led me straight into the hands of those who killed her. While running from them, I got lost in the lower levels and bumped into Sébastien. He helped me find the exit and made sure I was okay."

"Alix!" Sheer shock has taken over my sister's face.

"Oh, and Gaspar is dead. Always has been. Well, not always, but as long as I've known him." A surreal feeling of smugness spreads through me, as if everything I've just told her was part of some amazing experience that she missed out on.

In the rear-view mirror I can see Cédric watching me, but for once he's keeping his mouth shut. Meanwhile, Hélène has gone white as a sheet, her brown eyes wide with horror. "Is any of this true?" she whispers.

I cross my arms sullenly. "Yes. Do you need more details?"

"Alix. I don't know what to say." Preferably nothing, but that wouldn't be my sister. "You're going to stay away from them now, won't you?"

"Them?"

"The ghosts," she hisses, as if it's obvious. "They're obviously dangerous. You could have died."

"But not because of the ghosts! It was a real person who shot at me. A living person."

Hélène shakes her head. "Does it matter? You only got yourself into this situation because of the ghosts."

I can't believe her. She knows that ghosts are real now and she still thinks I've got a problem. "Emily was shot without knowing about the ghosts."

"Who is Emily?"

"The ghost whose murder I was investigating."

"You're not the police!" Hélène sounds incredulous. Then she nudges Cédric. "Tell her!"

Cédric looks as uncomfortable as I am. "You should've come to me."

Small chance. I sigh. "I wasn't aware that's what happened. She kept it from me."

Hélène gives a short bark. "Oh, that makes it so much better. You just followed a complete stranger—a *dead* stranger—into the catacombs. No wonder you got dragged into shady business like that."

She may have a point, but I'm sure as hell not going to give it to her. Especially when she doubles down.

"And, of course, you'd get yourself a dead boyfriend. Because that's totally on brand for you."

"Hélène..." Cédric of all people comes to my rescue.

She pauses for a moment, her eyes softening. "Are you okay?"

"Didn't you just establish that I'm not?" I ask in a hushed voice. Of course I'm not okay. I'm a total mess. And maybe I would've appreciated my big sister being there for me. But she isn't. She's just finding a new angle to assert her moral superiority over me.

Hélène sighs. "I'm sorry. This is all a bit much for me."

Oh, it's too much for *her*! This is ridiculous.

"Can we at least agree that you'll be more careful from now on? That you won't let these ghosts drag you into their dangerous schemes anymore?" Her eyes beg me to give her the promise she so desperately craves.

I can't. Not like this. "What about the police? Is it alright for Sébastien to drag me into this? He wants me to go back to the catacombs with him and lead him to the murder site."

Another gasp from my dear sister. "You can't seriously consider going back there."

"So now I can't trust the police either?" Look at me, pushing all her buttons.

Cédric keeps watching me through the mirror while Hélène has another fit. "You're being ridiculous, Alix, and you know it! Of course you should trust the police. But you're not a trained officer, and after what you just told me, you should be running in the opposite direction. Fast!"

"And forgo my civic duty?" I was more than sceptical before, but now I want to do it just for the sake of it. Sébastien thought I could do it. Why can't my dear old sister?

"Do you want me to come with you?" Cédric asks, calm and reassuring.

"Cédric!" my sister screeches. "Don't encourage her!"

"I'm not." He flashes her a quick smile. "I just want to make sure that Alix feels safe and supported. I'm sure if my cousin says it's safe enough to bring a civilian, she'll be fine. But it can still be scary." And now I'm the recipient of his smarmy smile. "I commend your bravery. It's just like I told you. You'd be perfect for this. But I know what it's like to bite off more than you can chew. So, whenever you need me, I'll be there for you."

I stare at him, completely perplexed. Have I been wrong about Cédric all this time? Is he actually a good guy? I still feel uncomfortable that he cares so much about me, but at least it's more than I get from my sister these days.

Speaking of my sister. She shoots him daggers with her eyes, a silent promise that they'll talk about it later. For the rest of the trip, she chews on it in silence.

When the car stops in front of our apartment, Hélène turns back to me. "Cédric is right. You can always come to us if you need help. Please do."

"Yeah, I don't think so." I grab my bag and open the car door.

Cédric gets out and takes my bike off the rack. "Give your sister some time. Her whole world has just turned upside down. She's just worried about you."

It's such a cheap excuse. As if worry absolves you of every insult. "I'd much rather have her support."

He hands me the bike. "You have mine."

Completely weirded out, I just stand there and watch him get back in the driver's side.

"Say hello to your parents for us." Before Cédric ducks his head, his face softens. "And I'm sorry about your boyfriend. I was looking forward to meeting him."

Dealing with Hélène has drained me even more. I should be getting on with my homework. Instead, I lift Malou out of her cage and rub her soft belly. She's rather sleepy this time of day but she doesn't mind the extra attention. Usually, she never fails to brighten my day. Not so today.

Tears fall from my eyes as my emotions once again overwhelm me. I can't believe what a mess my life has become. Hélène and I haven't been close for a long time, but just thinking about her makes me want to grind my teeth. That's my big sister. The one who asked me to be her witness. Could I have been nicer?

No, not at the moment. I don't feel capable of anything right now.

Ugh. I lay Malou on my stomach as I lie on my back and press the balls of my hands against my eyes. Thoughts and half-formed decisions swirl through my head: I'm afraid to return to the catacombs, but I want to go. Sébastien's face when he asked me to lead him. Cédric, who is his *freaking cousin*—and also offered to help. The Chevalier. Emily's dead body. And always Gaspar. My dead boyfriend.

A knock at the door startles me. I jump to my feet, accidentally disturbing Malou. The door opens, and my father sticks his head in. "Are you already—" His face changes as concern replaces the initial expression. "Have you been crying?"

My cheeks are still wet, so it's pretty obvious. "I'm fine."

He's not fooled in the least and decides to come in, closing the door gently behind him. "What happened?" He sits down on my bed, his feet close to where I'm lying on the floor.

Unable to answer that question in any useful detail, I go for deflection. "What are you doing home?"

"I handed in my exposé yesterday and took the day off." He smiles. "I basically slept until you got home."

"Was it that bad?"

"Nah, just a lot of late nights. I think I broke my brain trying to figure out the timeline," he jokes, then takes Malou out of my hands. "How's our little lady?"

"Great." Everyone in my family is in love with her. "She's a real hero, you know?"

When he raises an eyebrow, I realise I almost told him about the catacombs. But then I remember that my mother told me he was a bit of a cataphile himself in his youth. "She found us a way out of the catacombs after we got lost."

Sure. Technically, Sébastien told me how to get out, but Malou was already on her way.

"You went into the catacombs?"

"Are you going to tell me off as well?"

Frowning, he asks, "Who told you off? Marguerite?"

"Hélène."

"Ah." He sounds slightly amused. "I heard you two were having a bit of a row at the moment."

It's much more serious than that. "I'm exercising use of my right to remain silent." Once I start talking, my portrayal of Hélène won't be favourable.

My father laughs and throws up his hands. "I'm not going to get involved. But it sounds like your sister to forbid you. She wasn't born with a sense of adventure like you and me. Bit risk-adverse, that one."

"You can say *that* out loud. And controlling. And—" I stop myself before I go any further. "I guess she's just worried about me."

The amusement fades from my father's eyes. "Do we have to worry about you?"

"I'm fine, really."

"I'd be a pretty shitty journalist if I let you off the hook that easily."

"But you'd make a great papa!" My voice hiccups at the end.

He frowns, not trusting my fake cheerfulness. "Would I?"

The longer he holds my gaze, the harder it becomes not to cry. Words fight to be spoken, but I swallow them all. My father never bothered me much about the ghosts, but he didn't protest when my mother sent me to therapy. As far as I know, he has no idea how much my life revolves around them.

The last thing I want to do right now is explain everything that has happened. I can't bear another discussion about it today. I'd have to tell him all about Gaspar.

Gaspar.

He's at the root of this giant mess. The boyfriend I can never introduce to my father, never take to Hélène's wedding, never marry myself. There is no future for us, and yet for everyone else, there wasn't even a past.

My mind fixates on all the lost opportunities, the life I won't have. How do I explain all this heartache and grief for a boy I never knew? How do I avoid being asked about him all the time?

The answer is frighteningly simple. "Gaspar broke up with me!" I burst into tears as the lie rips from my throat.

"Oh, darling." My father pulls me close. I have no idea if he already knew about Gaspar, but it doesn't matter. He understands heartbreak. And my heart is broken into a million pieces.

CHAPTER 6

When I return to the Panthéon the next day, I feel only slightly better. Crying to my papa helped a little, but it doesn't solve the actual problem. Gaspar didn't break up with me. He died, but he's still here. And he's his usual sweet, charming, lovable self.

Unlike some of the older ghosts, Gaspar gives me space at work and doesn't interfere with my tours. When I look around, I find him sitting on the steps or leaning against the wall, watching me blissfully. Or he's in conversation with one of the other ghosts, learning about their fabulous lives.

When my shift is over and the Panthéon closes its doors, he comes to find me in the break room, away from prying eyes—dead or alive.

"I hope this isn't too awkward," he says as I close the door behind him. "Watching you at work?"

"I'm used to it." At least he will never correct me when I do my tour like everyone else.

Gaspar chuckles. "I bet you are. You're really good, by the way. If I were a tourist, I'd be very happy to join a tour of yours."

Blushing, I take off my work jacket and put it in the locker. No one has ever raved about my tours. Most people take you for granted. There are a few thanks, and American tourists always try to tip you, but otherwise there's very little praise—and a lot of criticism from the undead subjects of my tours.

"How are you settling in?" I ask, half hidden by my locker door as I change into my normal clothes.

Gaspar sits on the bench, not even trying to catch a glimpse of my underwear. "The ghosts are awesome. I still can't believe I talked to Pierre and Marie Curie or Jean-Jacques Rousseau." The excitement is slowly draining from his voice. "It's a wonderful place. I can see why you work here." His voice stops completely, and I can hear him taking a shaky breath. Like a living person.

"I'm truly grateful for everything you've done for me," he says at last.

"But?" I finish tying my scarf and close the locker door to look at him.

There's a sad little smile on his face as he looks at me. "I just wish I wasn't dead." He closes his eyes and takes another deep breath. It's a comforting gesture, one that older ghosts abandon since there's no real advantage in keeping up the pretence.

My heart goes out to Gaspar. I sit down next to him and take his hands in mine. "Me too."

Gaspar opens his eyes again and gives me the same pained smile as before. "Yeah. It sucks." He laughs, then lifts one of his hands to run it through my hair, draping it over my shoulder, as he stares at it longingly. "It's not really fair, is it? Why didn't I stay in bed longer that day? Or come in earlier to sit in the library? I could've taken the Métro or another route. We could've met somewhere else." He shuffles closer, his eyes suddenly full of passion. "In fact, I'm convinced we *would* have met somewhere else. Because you and me..." The passion fades as his gaze drops. "Well, I guess there can never really be a you and me."

My throat swells and I find it painful to swallow. When I first brought him here, it was all about settling him in, taking care of him. Now it's time to face up to what this means for us. For me. "It would certainly be a first for me."

He snorts. "And here I thought you only dated ghosts."

"I might as well," I admit. "Seeing ghosts isn't exactly endearing to most guys. The only person who believes in me and supports me is Gaby. Until I met you. But we both know that wasn't real."

"Oh, it was real," Gaspar claims. "I just happened to be a ghost at the time. But if we'd met before and you'd told me... I'd have found it very endearing. Metal," he adds with a wink.

I laugh for the first time in days. "Thanks. I needed that."

"You've cried a lot, haven't you?" He slides a little closer so that our legs touch. Before I can ask him how he knows, Gaspar says, "Your face is a bit puffy, your eyes are red. You still look beautiful, just exhausted."

I rest my head on his shoulder and sigh. "I really, really wanted this for us. You made me feel giddy and... happy."

Gaspar puts his fingers on my chin and turns my face towards him. "That doesn't have to stop, does it?"

It's so hard to resist when I look into his deep brown eyes. "I don't know how it can continue."

"What's really changed? Between us, I mean. You're still here. I'm still here. We can talk, laugh," his gaze falls on my lips, "kiss."

I can't resist the temptation. Gaspar is right. I can feel his warmth on my side, the soft touch of his skin against mine, and my stomach is still home to all those butterflies when he looks at me like that. I lean in and kiss him. My whole body is tense, expecting something to have changed, but his lips are as full as ever, his response as passionate as ever. To me, he's as real as they come.

The door opens suddenly, and I almost fall off the bench as I jump away from Gaspar. Breathing heavily, I look to see who has dared to come in after hours.

"Alix." Philippe sounds as surprised to find me here as I am to see him. "Are you okay?"

Flustered, I run my fingers through my hair. "Yes, sure. Why wouldn't I be?"

"Because it's half an hour after closing time, and you're still here." He narrows his eyes. "Besides, you look like I interrupted you at something."

"I was practising my talk for uni. It's quiet here. Usually."

Fortunately, he accepts my excuse and immediately lightens up. "That makes sense. I'll be out of your hair in a second. I just left something in my locker."

He searches his locker while I sit stiffly on the bench, not daring to check on Gaspar. After a minute that drags on like chewing gum, Philippe triumphantly holds up a thin gift box. "Got it! I'm not the worst boyfriend in history now."

"Just the most forgetful," I tease him gently.

Philippe grins. "Good luck with your talk." Then he rushes back out the door.

A little later I hear the lock on the side door click into place. Only then do I dare to turn back to Gaspar.

He's still sitting in the same place as before, grinning from ear to ear for some inexplicable reason. "Where were we?" he asks cheekily.

I feel like I'm going to be sick. My stomach turns at the thought of what would have happened if Philippe had seen me kissing the air. We're not exactly friends, but our relationship would be ruined forever. "I can't."

Gaspar frowns. "What do you mean?"

I stand up. "I can't do this with you. There's no point."

The words inadvertently cut into him. It's not what I wanted, and I feel sorry, but I can't take them back because it tears my own heart to pieces to say them.

"You don't exist for anyone but me." And Sébastien, although I doubt he's interested in validating my relationship. "I can never take you home to my parents. I can never introduce you to Gaby, who's been dying to meet you." I shake my head at the unfortunate choice of words and try to keep my composure as best as I can. "We have no future. We never had a past. And we can't have a present. I'm sorry."

And with that, I grab my bag and run out the room.

The November weather is as dreary as I feel. It's cold and drizzly and dark. The roads are wet, my light reflecting off a hundred puddles. I think about how Gaspar died in a cycling accident but shake the thought off because it only reminds me that he *has* died.

I lock my bike at one of the entrances to Père Lachaise and take out my phone to text Gaby that I've broken up with him. She asks if I'm alright, which makes me laugh. No, I'm not okay, but I have to be. I know that breaking up won't be enough. For my own sanity I should send him away, ask him to leave me alone. And maybe I will, some other day.

Don't worry. I'll be fine, I text back to Gaby.

Her reply comes promptly: *Well, if you need me, you know where I am.*

Thanks.

Due to the rain and the late hour, the cemetery is pretty deserted—at least if you only count the living. The ghosts don't mind the wet conditions and carry on with business as usual. I stop for a moment to listen to Chopin playing an unfamiliar piece, the notes ringing clearly from an instrument as ghostly as he is. When he notices me standing, he acknowledges me with a gentle smile. I applaud before moving on to my grandmother's lot.

She and Beatrice are entertaining Alexandre de Beauharnais, a revolutionary general who was guillotined during the Reign of Terror and the first husband of Napoleon's wife Joséphine. He's very gentlemanly and helped me a lot with my French Revolution assignments. His grave is in de Picpus on the other side of town, but he visits quite often. I'm almost a hundred percent sure he has a crush on my grandmother.

He takes his leave when I approach and nods at me. "Good evening, Mademoiselle Alix."

"Good evening." I wait until he's gone before I give my grandmother a sharp look.

She waves it off. "Oh, darling. He's much too young for me."

"He was born in 1760."

"But he died a young man."

I roll my eyes. "If you say so." At least ghosts can have any relationship they want.

"Besides, I've got Beatrice."

"I wouldn't mind sharing." Beatrice cackles and claps the top of her gravestone. "What brings you here on such a dreary day?" She shuffles over so that I can lean against the stone instead of sitting on the wet grass.

"I've just broken up with my boyfriend." At least that initial lie has become true now.

The two of them exchange a look. "Oh. Was that the young man you told us about last time."

Last time seems like ages ago, not weeks. "Yes."

"Did he turn out a rule-stickler in the end?" Beatrice sneers in distaste.

"Nope. But being with him would break all the rules." I let go of the tension in my shoulders and deflate. "He's dead. Always has been."

Nothing could have prepared me for my grandmother's reaction. "Oh, that's wonderful!"

"How?" I stare at her. "How could that possibly be wonderful?"

"Well, because we get to meet him." Her eyes light up with excitement.

I groan as I realise what she means. "But you're the only ones who can."

Beatrice pats my hand. "Oh, don't underestimate the number of ghosts that have taken an interest in your life."

Great, so I can share my relationship with the undead. As if my life wasn't already messed up enough.

My grandmother's face softens. "Do you love him?"

"It doesn't matter."

"Do you?" she insists.

I take a shaky breath. "Yes. Very much so," I announce for all the cemetery to hear.

"And is he a good boy? Does he treat you well?" She looks so serious.

"He's perfect," I admit. "Apart from being dead."

My grandmother smiles gently. "Would that really be so bad?"

"Um, yes." I can't believe I'm suddenly having to justify my choice. "I can't introduce him to anyone I know or spend mean-ingful time with him in any place with other people, which is pretty much everywhere. We can't go out on dates, and if I talk to him or touch him, it makes me look crazy. It's all a lie." Woah. Where did that rant come from? "I want someone who..." Sadness overwhelms me as I realise that I do want him. In spite of every-thing. "Someone I can be with. For real."

Beatrice puts her arms around me and hugs me tightly. "Oh, darling."

"The perfect man doesn't exist," my grandmother tells me in-stead. "But that doesn't mean you should give up on love."

"Grandma, please."

"He's here, love," she whispers. "At least I think that's him, judging by the heartbroken look on his face."

I whirl around, almost tripping over the gravestone. Sure enough, Gaspar has followed me here, looking like a lost puppy. He must have heard every word I just said. "Gaspar..."

Swallowing, he takes a tentative step forward. "I'm sorry." He stares at the ground. "I didn't mean to eavesdrop or cause you so much pain. I just..." He lifts his eyes to meet mine. "If you want me gone, I'll leave. But if you don't..." The words remain unspoken, holding such sweet promise.

"I don't," I admit, then shudder. Tears burn in my eyes, and I'm so tired of them. "I wish there was a way."

"Well, maybe there is," Beatrice whispers.

"How?" Unless she knows a way to bring Gaspar back to life, I don't see much hope for us.

"Ask Abelard and Héloïse," my grandmother says with steely determination. Then she shoos us away. "Go at once. Both of you."

I have no idea what the point of all this is, but since my protests are falling on deaf ears, I might as well give it a try. Crossing my arms, I make my way up the hill to where the famous tomb is located.

Gaspar jogs up beside me, glancing over his shoulder. "Who are Abelard and Héloïse?"

"You don't know?" When he shakes his head, I explain. "Famous lovers who were separated by evil forces but remained true to each other." He raises his eyebrows and I chuckle. The notion is ridiculous. Gaspar and I have nothing in common with Abelard and Héloïse. Nevertheless, I continue, "They were married in the Middle Ages, both ahead of their time, very intelligent, and sought after for their ideas. But Héloïse's uncle wasn't a fan of Abelard, or there were some misunderstandings—depends on who's telling the story. Fact is, he thought Abelard had shamed his niece, and organised some thugs to assault and castrate him."

Next to me, Gaspar winces. It's probably not a man's favourite story.

I shrug. "Abelard decided to enter a monastery and Héloïse was stuck in a convent. They continued to write love letters to each other but never saw each other again." If I were a tour guide at Père Lachaise, I would romanticise the story more, but the truth is there were only six letters—albeit very passionate ones—and their romantic relationship has been exaggerated by later poets and playwrights, when in fact their time together pales in comparison to all the individual achievements they made.

"So, like Romeo and Juliet?" Gaspar asks, his lips quirking up a little.

"With castration."

He laughs. "Beats dying."

I sigh heavily. It probably does. Abelard suffered a horrible fate, but it wasn't the end of his life. He continued to teach and influence, becoming one of the most renowned philosophers of his time, and perhaps the forefather of universities. And Héloïse was incredibly well-educated, a physician, and an early feminist. There's a reason we still know about them, even though they've been dead for nearly a thousand years.

Shyly, Gaspar slides a hand into mine. "It's not the end of the world, you know? Dying."

Maybe I'm being unfair. I've known for years that ghosts have a rich afterlife. It's what I love about them and why I'm not afraid of death when it comes. But society isn't exactly on my side, as evidenced by Hélène's protests or Théo's arguments in class.

Gaspar groans. "Oh god, that sounded like I was suggesting death to you. No, absolutely not. Don't even think about it!"

"I'm not." I love ghosts, but I'm not ready to become one.

Satisfied, he nods. "I'm slowly wrapping my head around it, that with everything I see and experience, my life—no, my existence—isn't over yet. I'm still here."

I squeeze his fingers in sympathy. While I'm here crying about losing him before I had the chance to fall in love with him, Gaspar is grappling with a literally life-changing turn of events. "It's really not that bad, as far as I know."

"Apart from that," he mumbles, looking at our hands.

In response, I let go of him and avert my eyes.

We've reached the top of the hill where the tomb of the medieval lovers lies. It's separated from the rest of the tombs by a black wrought-iron fence. Inside is a chapel-like crypt open on all sides where the stone figures of Héloïse and Abelard lie side by side. Of course, the ghosts themselves aren't lying around but strolling around their little garden, deep in conversation.

"Good evening," I say loudly to get their attention. My hands wrap around the spearheads ends of the fence. The coldness of the metal biting into my palms keeps my mind sharp.

"Alix!" Héloïse exclaims in delight as they both come over. "It's been a while since you last visited."

We don't have a close relationship, but of course I've done my research. "Yes, well, um... this is Gaspar."

They look at him with interest and a little confusion. They're probably wondering why I'm introducing them to a ghost.

"Hi." Gaspar flashes a quick smile. "We were sent up here because apparently you two give love advice."

My face flushes with heat and I could sink into the ground. "Gaspar!"

"What? That's why, isn't it?" He smiles at the old couple again. "You see, Alix and I would love nothing more than to be together, but there's this little problem. I'm dead, she's not. Which is a good thing," he adds, as if on cue.

"Oh no!" Héloïse seems shocked. "What happened? Did someone go after you?"

"No, just a normal accident. Pretty boring when you think about it," Gaspar quips, but then his face can no longer hide the pain. "I still don't know what I'm supposed to do now. Can't exactly join a monastery. Can I?"

Abelard chuckles softly. After nine hundred years, he's no longer offended by the mention of his ghastly fate. "Are you here for advice on love or death?"

Gaspar and I share a look and his face softens again. "Is there any hope for us?"

"Well, I don't see why not." Héloïse sounds rather casual. "If you ask me, it's rather ideal."

Sometimes ghosts really confuse me. "Ideal how?"

"Well, think about it. There are no consequences. You could have him as much as you like, and no one would be the wiser. Besides, you won't find yourself pregnant."

I should've known better than to ask these two about matters of love. Abelard and Héloïse are famous for their racy and not at all time-appropriate relationship. They had sex everywhere, even in church. My face burns as my mind happily jumps ahead and imagines having sex with Gaspar. With a ghost! "No, absolutely not," I stutter.

Gaspar blinks quite often. The poor guy looks shocked. Considering that five minutes ago he had no idea who Abelard and Héloïse were, it's not surprising. "You can have sex as a ghost?"

"If you're not incapacitated," Abelard says through his teeth.

Héloïse melts into his side and comforts him. "It's possible, but that's not what's important, is it?"

"Right." Abelard nods. "If you want my advice, forget it before you get in too deep. It's not easy to keep a love alive when circumstances separate you." And with this gloomy advice, Abelard turns away and makes his way to the other side of their garden.

Héloïse sighs. "Don't mind him. He's going through one of his phases. They happen every century."

"I thought the two of you were happy now that you're together." Obviously, life was tough for them, but their remains were buried together for a long time. After a comparatively short life spent apart, they had half an eternity together in death.

"We are lucky to have each other." Héloïse smiles sadly. "And sometimes that's enough. But Abelard lost so much. When it became known that he'd married me and we'd had a child, his reputation took a beating. And of course, my uncle ordered that heinous act. I never wanted to marry him in the first place."

Gaspar looks up in confusion. "I thought you loved him."

"You can love someone without being bound by marriage. Marriage was only for my benefit, and little of that, but it was always to his detriment. We were happiest before we took our vows, and I wouldn't have minded being his mistress. Instead, we spent a lifetime apart." She glances over her shoulder at Abelard. "But what really ails him is the loss of our son."

I never bothered to find out what happened to the child she gave birth to, as he wasn't a prominent figure in their tale.

"Abelard would have given up everything, his reputation, his disciples, to live a small life with me and our son, but it wouldn't have been right. He was destined for more, and I wasn't willing to dim his light, so we gave Astrolabe to his sister to raise. He led a quiet life and has long since passed on."

"You mean you never met him in the afterlife?"

Héloïse shakes her head. "Not even once."

My heart aches for her and Abelard. Their story is well-known, and every day, people come here to leave their love letters in memory of their famous affair. But the people they grew up with, their family, all that is long gone. That's the fate of most ghosts. Even this existence is limited.

"Abelard longs for everything we never had. He has me, but there's a child-size hole in his heart." She looks at Gaspar and me, her gaze full of warmth. "But don't let our fate determine yours. You live... well, exist, in another world, a much more open world. Experiment. Explore. What have you really got to lose?"

"Her reputation," Gaspar says before I can even entertain the idea. He looks so serious right now. "I don't want to hang on to Alix if my presence tarnishes her life. I like her too much for that." He turns to me, searching my horrified gaze. "Saying that, I've found out what I want to do with my afterlife now."

"You have?" My voice does a somersault through the words. Obviously, he took a completely different message from Abelard and Héloïse's heartbreak. Just as I'm warming to the idea of giving us a chance, he pulls back.

With a serious look in his eyes, he nods. "Yes. We may not have a future together, but I can help you, support you, be your constant friend." When I don't react immediately, he elaborates. "I can go places you can't, protect you as best as I can."

His words remind me of what Sébastien said yesterday. About how GoPol uses ghosts to spy for them. I don't ever want to think of Gaspar as a tool to be used by me, but the idea of having a devoted ghost friend has its merits. A love affair might be too out there, but I could use a companion. Especially if I have to return to the catacombs.

"I'd like that very much," I whisper at last.

And there it is, that beautiful smile that made me fall in love with him in the first place. "Then it's a deal." Gaspar laughs and gives me an elaborate bow. "I will be your faithful servant."

Chapter 7

Three days later, I meet Sébastien at the hidden entrance under the abandoned Métro station with Gaspar in tow. The policeman doesn't bat an eyelid at Gaspar's presence and nods to him as if he were an old friend. "You must be Alix's ghost friend."

I appreciate that he doesn't call him my boyfriend, although it grates on me that he immediately recognises Gaspar as a ghost. Nevertheless, I make the necessary introductions, and we all head off into the catacombs.

My heart pounds as we enter the ancient tunnels. The last time I was here, I was chased by a madwoman with a gun. I've underestimated the power of these memories returning all at once. When I walked through it, it was through the pale beam of my mobile phone. In the light, this lower level of the catacombs gives me a delayed panic. I can see piles of crumbled stone, broken walls, and deep holes leading off into the void. It's a miracle I haven't broken a leg or worse while I was here.

None of us speak as Sébastien leads the way. I would've had no idea where to go as I only paid attention to Malou last time, but he finds the big pile of rubble I'd slid down. He shines his torch on the upper floor. "That's where you came down."

We crawl up the pile on all fours. The rubble slides under my feet, but Gaspar is right there to hold me whenever I slip. At the top, Sébastien pulls himself up as if it were nothing, while I need both of their help to get to the top.

Sébastien points the beam down the corridor. "I found your rucksack about sixty metres down that way. When we get there, you'll have to take over."

I take a deep breath, unsure if I can do it. Then again, if I remember correctly, we only ran in one direction, not bothering with any side tunnels. It should be easy enough to get to the place with the water.

In the end, Gaspar and I *took* two turns, but together we identify them easily and manage to find the water corridor. "To get to the place, we have to crawl through this, then climb down a well, and through a narrow window." I swallow as I face the water. "This is where they were waiting for us."

Gaspar puts a hand on my shoulder. "I'll stay here. If anyone comes, I can warn you."

Sébastien nods. "Good plan." He offers me the lead with a small bow.

I look at Gaspar. "Be careful."

"I'm a ghost."

"He had a ghost whisperer last time. She saw both of us." If she hadn't, I never would have got away.

Gaspar shrugs. "But she can't hurt me. I mean what is she going to do? Kill me?"

I don't like it, but he's got a point. It's me who needs protecting, not him. He's already lost everything.

Sébastien waits patiently for me to say goodbye before following me down the flooded tunnel. He doesn't speak until we're much further down and almost forced to crawl on all fours. "So, is he the only ghost you have a close relationship with?"

Close relationships, that's one way of putting it. "No, I have many dead friends." Only with Sébastien does that sound even remotely normal.

"Many?"

"I work at the Panthéon. And I often visit the cemeteries."

"Why?" Sébastien sounds surprised.

I lower my head even more, dreading the moment when I'll have to immerse myself completely in the water. "Why not?" As a ghost whisperer, I wouldn't have expected him to balk at that.

"Isn't it a bit weird?"

Oh dear. I thought *he* of all people would understand. "They're just people. My world would be much poorer without their presence in my life."

As I look back over my shoulder, his face is strangely distorted. He tries to straighten it out when he catches my stare. "I guess in a way they are."

"Don't you spend any time with ghosts?" The ceiling is so low now that I can no longer escape the water.

"Not outside of work. Then again, my cousin would probably say I don't spend time with anyone."

His cousin, my future brother-in-law. "Is that true?"

"Only because I'm committed to my work."

"So, you're a workaholic?"

"I suppose so."

"But you don't hang out with ghosts?"

"Not usually, no."

What a sad and empty life. I know people think I'm a loner because I only have Gaby, but that couldn't be further from the truth. I have so many friends who just aren't visible to everyone else.

I feel cold. Maybe *I'm* the one who leads a sad life. This whole thing with Gaspar is just the culmination of more than a decade of preferring ghosts to people. It's like everything Hélène ever said is true. The thought makes me so sick I want to throw up.

"Is there a problem?" Sébastien sounds tense. Ready to attack, I suppose.

Nervously, I continue to crawl. "No, everything's fine." Just the realisation that my life is a sham. I should be out there, partying with friends, doing stupid shit, and enjoying life. Instead, I'm crawling through this horrible passage, thinking about ghosts.

I spend the rest of the way in silence. Finally, the water recedes, and we reach the bone well. I point to it. "We have to go down here and then through a window at the bottom. It has a bend at the end, so don't panic when you reach it."

Sébastien raises an eyebrow. Then he says in a deadpan voice. "I won't panic."

"Well then, officer." I invite him to go first.

He scoffs at my disrespectful tone but doesn't comment, instead lowering himself into the well. I have little interest in revisiting Ossa Arida myself. The alternative would be to stay here alone with the bones, and that's no better, so I follow him down the well and through the window.

Like last time, the last passage is the worst. It's a little better when you know what to expect, but it's simply too narrow for comfort, and my heart jumps in my throat when I hit the bend in the tunnel, even though I know it's coming.

When I pull myself out, Sébastien is just standing there. "Where to next?"

"What do you—?" I catch myself.

When Emily led me here, the floor was littered with bones—and Emily's dead body—and there was a gruesome altar on the upper floor. Now the room has been swept so thoroughly not a single splinter remains. For a moment I fear I've led Sébastien to the wrong place, but then again, how many other water-filled tunnels lead to the exact same well and window? No, this room has been altered.

I show Sébastien the pictures on my phone again. "It looked like this."

"Hmm." He barely acknowledges me and goes up the stairs to the upper floor. I see him bend down and study the stone beneath his feet.

Curious, I follow him up. Someone has sprayed graffiti on the floor. "Ne cherchez pas." *Don't search.*

A shiver runs down my spine. They knew we would come back here.

"Looks like they moved their operations." Sébastien sounds disappointed.

He stands and shines his light into the tunnel leading out of the room. I follow him as quietly as I can, afraid someone will jump out at us. But the tunnel remains empty, leading to a dead end, not a window in sight.

"Up there." Sébastien points the light above our heads. Beyond our reach is another well that seems to go up and up and up into the darkness. He studies the stone again and shows me two scratched indentations. "They had a ladder to get in and out. There's no way we can follow them."

I'm glad he's not suggesting we climb up there, but I can't help feeling disappointed. "So, this is where it ends? We're just going to stop?"

He turns to look at me. "You've done as much as I asked. Thanks for that. We should go back now."

"What do you mean?" I stare at him in disbelief. "Are you going to investigate this further? Are you cutting me out? Or are you giving up on the case?" *Are you giving up on me?* The words pop into my head, unbidden and confusing. I've only just met the guy.

"What I do is none of your business." His face softens slightly. "You're a civilian, Alix. I needed you to lead me here, but the rest is up to GoPol."

"So, you're done with me?" I don't know why that's such a big deal. Everything Sébastien said makes perfect sense. Now I can go back to my boring life full of dead people that no one else can see. And that's when I get it. Sébastien is like me. He's the first decent person I've met with the same ability, but he has no interest in taking it any further, because he doesn't need me. But I need him.

Sébastien looks a little uncomfortable. I'm obviously being ridiculous. "I'm not *done* with you. Our relatives are getting married, so we'll see each other."

What a cop-out. As if we don't both know that we're planning to stay as far away from this wedding as possible. "Sure. Sorry, you just caught me off guard." Like everything else lately.

I don't wait for him to explain any more, and head back to the small passage. Now that I'm going through it for the fourth time, it's really just a strenuous exercise, nothing more. But as soon as I pull myself up, I get a terrible shock.

A huge figure is standing on the other side, waiting for me. *Literally.* "Mademoiselle Alix."

It takes me a moment to calm my racing heart and recognise the man. "Grand Master Molay!" It's the Knight Templar I met in the Boutique de la Psychose. The one who sent me running with a taste of schizophrenia I never want to repeat.

"It's been ten days."

I swallow hard. "I'm sorry." It's all coming back to me now. I was supposed to introduce him to the ghosts of the Panthéon, something I'd completely forgotten after all the drama with Gaspar.

"When?" he asks in a commanding tone.

"Tomorrow. I'm back at work tomorrow. I'll ask them then." It's such a small favour, and if it keeps me from being stalked and scared half to death, I'm keen to be done with it.

Molay nods at me. "See that you do."

"Do you need help?"

I whirl around as another voice joins our conversation. At first I think it's Sébastien's voice, but although it's similar, this guy sounds more cheerful. And yet...

My light shines into his startling blue eyes. He blinks in annoyance and scowls, looking *exactly* like Sébastien and yet different. The guy before me is a teenager. There's no trace of a beard and he's wearing nothing but tracksuit bottoms and a black T-shirt, as if he'd come jogging rather than climbing through the tunnel. Speaking of which, the trousers are dry. Even if the fabric dries quickly, it should at least be muddy. Add to that the more than inappropriate outfit for catacomb crawling.

This guy isn't alive. "Who are you?"

"Dix-Sept, but you can call me Dix. Séb does, to avoid the confusion."

I have no idea what he's talking about, but there's an old Templar who needs attention. I turn around to see that he's gone. Delivering his message was apparently all he wanted to do.

"Your ghost isn't very good at taking care of you, is she?" Dix asks nonchalantly.

"My ghost? He's keeping watch at the end of the passageway, though I doubt Molay used it that way." The Grand Master probably knows the catacombs better than anyone.

Dix raises his eyebrows, looking so disturbingly like my new officer friend that I shudder. Something sinister is afoot. "He?"

"Yes, Gaspar is a he."

"Oh, I don't mean *him*. He's a good little soldier, just very inexperienced." Dix smiles, for once not looking like Sébastien at all. "I meant *your* ghost. Little Alix. From when you died."

CHAPTER 8

I blink once. Twice. My brain short-circuits as I try to make sense of even ten percent of what Dix has just implied.

Before I think of an answer, Sébastien pulls himself out of the window. He immediately scowls at Dix. "What are you doing here?"

"Saving Alix from the big bad wolf."

He talks about me as if we've been together for ages. He's embarrassing me too. "That man was Jacques de Molay, the last Grand Master of the Knights Templar. We've met."

Dix seems impressed, but Sébastien is annoyed. "Was she in any real danger?"

"No," I say at the same time as Dix quips, "Could have been."

Now I'm annoyed. Why are we even talking about this when there's something much bigger going on? "I wasn't. Now, let me ask you again. *Who* are you?"

Seeing the two of them side by side is like seeing double. Dix could be Sébastien's twin, if he weren't a few years younger and much more casual than the stuck-up officer. There's a conclusion here that's just too terrible to assume. I need *them* to confirm it.

Sébastien sighs. "Dix-Sept is my ghost. My eternal teenage self, so to speak." Without further explanation, he turns to Dix. "I'll take care of this. You go through that wall and up the well at the end of the room. I want you to find out as much as you can about where they've moved their operations to."

Dix gives him a mock salute. "Aye, aye, sir!" He gives me one last grin before fading backwards into the wall.

"He's such a nuisance."

I don't buy it. This casualness, as if I shouldn't be surprised—or *horrified*—that he's hanging out with his younger self. That he *died!* How is that even possible? I have so many questions, but they all seem to have to wait.

"Let's go back to the station. Please."

"Will you tell me everything?" I ask, half planning to stay here if he doesn't promise.

His shoulders sag. "Yes. Yes, I will."

And with that, he starts climbing up the bone well.

I follow him, still annoyed. Once again, we don't speak until we emerge from the water. There's no nasty surprise waiting for us, just Gaspar, who's happy to see us.

"That was quick."

"The place was empty," I explain.

Meanwhile, Sébastien looks around. "Did anyone come by?"

"Not a living soul."

An eyebrow rises. "And dead souls?"

Gaspar deflates slightly. "I didn't see any."

I'm reminded that Dix called Gaspar inexperienced and that he didn't see Molay or Dix approach me. I wonder if they ever used this tunnel—and *how* they knew I would be there. Obviously, I've still got a lot to learn about the afterlife.

But as far as I'm concerned, Gaspar's done his best. After all, it's not the ghosts I'm worried about, it's the living, breathing people like me. I slip my hand into his. "Let's go back."

Sébastien glances at our clasped hands but keeps his thoughts to himself. Together we walk back to the station.

As usual, the light is blinding after the darkness of the catacombs. There are only a few fluorescent lights down here, but it might as well be daylight. According to my mobile phone, it's around nine o'clock.

Sébastien and I sit on a graffiti-covered bench to talk. Gaspar sits on the other side of me, still holding my hand. For a moment it looks as if Sébastien is going to ask him to stay away, but then he must have realised that I'm only going to tell Gaspar what he said later anyway.

"About Dix..." Sébastien now avoids my gaze and clasps his hands between his knees as he stares at the floor. "I had a near-death experience when I was seventeen. All ghost whisperers do."

"All ghost whisperers have a near-death experience when they're seventeen?" I certainly hadn't.

"No, at any age." He looks up. "You don't know, do you?"

"Know what?"

"What makes you a ghost whisperer." He sounds genuinely surprised.

My veins turn to ice. Gaspar squeezes my hand, sensing my unease. "What makes *me* a ghost whisperer?"

Sébastien turns to me, scrutinising my face as if to accuse me of lying. "You must have been very young then."

"What *are* you talking about?" All these half-truths and insinuations make my skin crawl.

He straightens his shoulders. "Alright. Here's the thing. The reason you can see ghosts is because you had a brush with death. For however short a time, your heart stopped. You became a ghost, but then you were revived and lived on, making you a ghost whisperer. There are two of you. One dead, one alive. One foot in each world."

It all makes frightening sense—except for one thing. "I never had to be revived."

"You were probably too young to remember. But it happened. Trust me. Somewhere out there is a little ghost who used to be you."

I shudder to think of my childhood self as a ghost, separated from her family, all alone.

Sébastien is still studying my face. "You've never met her? She doesn't follow you around?"

"Is that what Dix does? Follow you around?" I'm not sure I'd want that; a constant reminder of my own mortality.

"He works with me, yes." Sébastien rubs his chin, looking uncomfortable. "I told you how we use ghosts to spy at GoPol. Well, we mostly use our own ghosts. They're the most reliable and able to influence the living world a bit."

"They are?" I've never heard of a ghost being able to do that.

Sébastien winces. "At least half of all reported hauntings are due to this kind of ghost."

"What about the other half?"

"Fake. Overactive imagination. Marketing."

"Oh." As interesting as this is, my thoughts circle back to my own ghost. "So, you think I died?"

"One hundred percent. It's the only way to become a ghost whisperer."

It takes me a few moments to process the information. It's not every day you're told that you died. I still can't quite believe it. Shouldn't I know if I had a near-fatal accident? How could I not?

Even if I'd been too young, surely, my parents would have told me the story at some point. And I've never met a little girl who looked like me. Sébastien must be wrong. He has to be.

"So," Gaspar asks quietly, "if I'd been revived at the scene of my accident, I would have been like you guys? Apart from being alive."

I squeeze his hand. It's a good reminder that even if this happened, I lived through it. You could even say that my life is richer for it. At least as far as I am concerned.

Sébastien nods curtly. "That's how it works."

"What about you?" I ask, suddenly worried about him. Unlike me, Sébastien was old enough to remember his temporary death.

"What about me?" He looks genuinely confused.

"How did it happen to you?" Is that insensitive? It can't be, not when we often talk to ghosts, and such.

Sébastien shrugs. "My heart stopped. It got restarted. Done."

I squint at him. That's such an evasive answer. I suppose I can't force him to talk about his death if he doesn't want to. He might still be traumatised by it. But... "Didn't you say you grew up around ghosts? That your father is also a ghost whisperer?"

"Yes, but I wasn't a ghost whisperer myself until then," he admits frankly. "So, when it happened, I was prepared for it."

I can't decide whether he was traumatised or admirably took it in his stride. It's probably none of my business. He seems to be well adjusted. Or maybe not, when I think of him and Dix standing next to each other. Sébastien is so serious, while Dix acted like a happy-go-lucky teenager with a bit of a rebellious streak. If they didn't literally look like each other, I would never have guessed that they were the same person.

I shudder at the thought. A ghost whisperer is a person split in two. Sébastien's ghost is literally called Dix-Sept, seventeen, for the age he died. And somewhere out there is a little Deus or Trois, or worse. A part that has split from me, permanently trapped in an age of little communication and overwhelming emotions. A sad existence, but also a missing part of myself.

"You'll find her, won't you?" Sébastien's blue eyes bore into me, and I realise he wants me to be reunited with my ghost. Maybe that connection is all I need to regain my balance between this world and the next.

"I'll have to try."

"Well, let me know when you do. I can help." He nods before getting up from the bench. "Alright. Let's get you home."

"What about Dix?" His ghost still hasn't emerged from the catacombs.

Sébastien shrugs, unconcerned. "He'll find me later."

"Aren't you worried?"

"About what? He's a ghost." Sébastien seems to find my concern amusing. "Don't worry. He may be seventeen forever, but he's been doing this job as long as I have. Dix is fine. He always is."

But Sébastien isn't. It's a thought I keep to myself as I follow him up the stairs and out into the dark November night.

CHAPTER 9

Sébastien drops me and Gaspar off at home, promising to let me know if he makes any progress on the Ossa Arida case. It's raining quite heavily as I get out of his car and run to the door. It's only when I'm in the hallway that I realise Gaspar has followed me here.

"What are you doing?" Not that I mind him being here—we haven't had a chance to talk yet—but I've become acutely aware that I've never had a boy over before. My relationships just never went far enough.

"I thought you could use a friend after what you heard down there." Gaspar holds up his hands in apology. "If you'd rather be alone, I'll go back to the Panthéon."

I take a moment to consider. My family is waiting for me upstairs, though by this time they'll probably be getting ready for bed. All the things I've just learned are things I can't tell them, not without raising serious concerns that I need to go back to therapy. And as comforting as it is to rub Malou's tummy, she can't really give any advice. Gaspar can.

"Fine, but you're not staying the night."

He chuckles. "Understood."

My heart aches as I allow myself to entertain the idea of us again. I would love to sneak my boyfriend up—something I didn't even know I wanted until now—but he's dead and I'm alive and we can never be.

Upstairs, my parents are still in the living room, watching an art movie by candlelight. I point to my room for Gaspar, before showing my face to my family for a moment. "I'm home."

My mother smiles at me. "Did you have a good time?"

Yeah, until they told me I almost died as a child. You wouldn't know anything about that, would you? The words burn my tongue and I feel my lips curl into in a fake smile. "It was good, yes." Neither of us bother to suggest what I spent my Friday night with.

Papa nods at me. "I'm glad you're feeling better."

"Somewhat."

"Oh, why would you say that?" Maman asks, but I leave them alone, not wanting to hear my father explain how I broke up with Gaspar.

Especially not when he's waiting in my room, where he's discovered Malou. My little hedgehog is wide awake and has been doing circles in her cage, but now she's curiously sniffing around the edge, where Gaspar is crouching and smiling at her.

"She knows I'm here," he whispers in awe.

I cross the distance between us and open the cage to pick her up. Malou can absolutely sense him. As soon as I put her on my knees, her little nose searches for Gaspar, who coos at her with delight. My hedgehog boy.

Wiping an errant tear from my cheek, I explain, "She's practically a ghost sniffer, my partner in crime."

Gaspar laughs, and I notice that it's the first time he's looked truly carefree since I confronted him near the Seine. "She's adorable. Can I touch her?"

"I don't know," I admit. Since Malou is still happy to stay relatively still, I cradle her and present her soft belly to Gaspar.

It's almost as if the world has stopped spinning for a moment and we are suspended in time. I watch as Gaspar's finger approaches Malou, hesitates for a tiny moment before sinking into her soft fur. "And?" I whisper.

"So soft." A broad smile spreads across his lips as he begins to spoil Malou rotten.

Malou relaxes in my hands, half-closing her eyes as she enjoys the attention, and I'm falling in love with Gaspar all over again.

He looks up at me and his smile falters. "Hey, what's wrong?"

I didn't even realise I was crying until he looked at me. Gaspar wraps his arms around me and pulls my head onto on his shoulder.

Malou slips out of my hands and makes her way around the room while I sniffle into Gaspar's embrace. He knows exactly what's wrong and doesn't need an answer.

"It's going to be alright," he mutters into my hair. In an even lower voice he adds, "I'm sorry I can't be what you need."

"You're dead!" I burst out in a strange accusatory tone as I push away from him. "What I mean is, don't apologise when you have it so much worse."

Gaspar shrugs helplessly. "Have I? Obviously, this wasn't what I had planned. I wanted to live a long, long life, but I also always thought that this life was the only one we had, that you had to make the most of it. And it's not. There is an afterlife, and it's not too bad, all things considered. At least so far. The thing that sucks the most at the moment is that I can't be there for you. That we only met now. That all I can do is watch you grieve for a guy you didn't even know." He smiles sadly. "You're probably grieving more than anyone who *knew* me."

"That's not true," I whisper through a tightening throat. "You have Gustave and Marie. They're devastated. And I'm sure your parents—"

He huffs, and I stop. With a sigh, he explains his reaction, "My parents are probably happy. Not *happy* happy, of course, but they'll pat themselves on the back and claim they always knew I'd end up like this."

"What? Why?" I know I've had my share of family problems, but they would be absolutely devastated if I died tomorrow. Even Hélène.

"They're just really stuck up. Got a lot of money and a lot of attitude." Gaspar's voice becomes nasal. "You're ruining our reputation." He rolls his eyes. "I've always been a bit of a rebel, and well," he shows me his black-painted fingernails and grins, "they don't like my style. Plus, they half-thought I was a Satanist because of the band shirts I wore. Would drive my mother mad. She tried to burn them once."

"No way!" I have to admit, they sound pretty awful. Poor Gaspar.

He shrugs again, as if none of this matters. "They also disapproved of my choice of studies. My father calls me a socialist instead of a sociologist, so there's that." He laugh softly. "I should've studied law like Marie or economics. Something to make money. Well, now they'll never have to live through the days I'd be an underpaid social worker, putting all my time and effort into projects that don't pay, serving underprivileged communities. The horror!"

Once again, I'm crying. I can't help it. All this potential taken from the world too soon. They say only the good die young, but it sucks. Especially, for me because with every word he says, I love him more. "They sound terrible. Like really, really, utterly terrible." At least I'll never have to meet them.

The door to my room opens, and Odile sticks her head in, looking horrified. "Who are you talking to?"

My first instinct is to say Gaby, but she sees I'm not on the phone. "I'm just talking to Malou."

Odile crosses her arms. "Are you? I heard you say something about being dead. Malou looks fine to me."

I stand up to close the door in my sister's face. "And she'll be fine. Now go to sleep or back to your phone. I have to call Gaby," I add, so she won't question me about talking at night.

But before I can close the door, Odile's sudden stare catches me off-guard. "Why are you crying?"

A fist-sized stone makes itself comfortable in my stomach. I've to swallow hard before I can say the words. "Because Gaspar and I have split up. Now go!"

Despite the softening of her face, I close the door, unwilling to confront her any further. For a few moments, I stand there, breathing in and out, trying to regain control of myself. When I turn around, Gaspar looks at me apologetically. "Sorry."

"I said don't," I whisper. "Not for that."

Annoyed at myself, I wipe my tears and distract myself with refilling Malou's food bowl and cleaning out her cage. Meanwhile, my little hedgehog is curious about Gaspar's scent in our room. She's got her front paws on his leg and is wrinkling her nose.

"She's such a cutie," Gaspar muses.

"Yeah." At least someone I care about can enjoy his presence. Animals are just something else.

Feeling a little better, I retreat to the side of the room that's the farthest from the wall I share with Odile, where my bed happens to be. I sit on it and tentatively tap on the mattress beside me, taking out my phone as an emergency alibi. Gaspar gets up from the floor, gently picks up Malou and joins me. He obviously enjoys interacting with a living creature, and it both warms and pains my heart to see them together.

As an extra precaution, I keep my voice as low as possible. "My family are lovely, but they don't know about the ghosts."

"You never told them?"

"I have. I first understood I was seeing ghosts when I was seven and we were burying my grandmother. I told my maman then, but she dismissed it as my imagination. When I kept seeing them, she booked me in to see a grief counsellor, thinking that's where it was coming from, so I kept it to myself and only trusted my big sister. She loved my ghost stories. Hélène and I used to go to the cemeteries together and she'd ask me, 'What about this person? What about that one?' And I had to talk to the ghosts and then tell her all about it."

The memory makes me smile. We were so close then. Just the two of us and the ghosts. What fun we had exploring. She even helped me with some of the favours.

"But then puberty struck, and Hélène outgrew it. One day she just decided that we were just playing pretend, that none of it was real. And because she had decided, I had to stop too." I sigh. It only got worse from there. "So, I stopped telling her. Or anyone. Until Gaby."

"That's your best friend, right?" Gaspar asks.

I nod. "Yeah, she's the best. It took her a while to get on board, but I was able to prove myself to her and she's been my biggest supporter ever since. I told her about you. She was super disappointed that you weren't... alive."

"Aren't we all?"

"Yeah." No, I'm not going to cry about it again. I've shed enough tears. It's time to get my life—and Gaspar's afterlife—back under control. And to do that, I apparently need to find out more about my own death. I shudder just thinking about it.

"So, Sébastien," Gaspar begins, seemingly having the same thoughts. "Will you continue to see him?"

Okay, maybe we're not thinking the same thing. "What do you mean?"

"Just curious. He's like you."

"He's *nothing* like me. The only thing we have in common is the ability to see ghosts."

Before I can continue with a list of differences, Gaspar interjects, "Which is a pretty big thing in your life."

"What are you implying? That I *like* him?" The thought hadn't even occurred to me.

Gaspar shrugs. "Just saying. He seems like a good egg. He understands you on a level no one else can. He's not bad looking, and most importantly, he's alive."

"I like *you!*" Why should he start hyping up this other guy I literally just met?

He winces as if I have suddenly declared my undying love for him. "And I like you too, but you said so yourself. You don't want to be with me. You can't."

"Well, yes. But that doesn't mean I have to throw myself at the next person who's barely decent. For all I know, Sébastien isn't even single. Besides, he's Officer Cédric's cousin—my sister's creepy fiancé—and that would be a 'no freaking way'."

Gaspar smiles. Suddenly he seems much more relaxed. "Okay. I just wanted to put it out there. For the future."

I can't help myself. I wrap my arms around his and lean my head on his shoulder, snuggling close. Everything about Gaspar feels so real, so tangible. The truth is I'm nowhere near ready to move on. No matter what reason says, I want to be with him. No one else.

"You have nothing to worry about," I say after a while. "As Sébastien said, I'm *not* part of the police. He doesn't need my help anymore, so I don't think we'll see much of each other, except from future family gatherings."

"Really?" Gaspar sounds sceptical. "You'd throw away your chance to get to know the one person who's familiar with your powers?"

When I followed Emily into the catacombs, I did so partly because I wanted to find other ghost whisperers. Now I have. "Well, I can't exactly ask him to hang out with me? He'd *definitely* take that the wrong way. Besides, you don't like it."

Gaspar scoffs, amused. "Don't listen to me. I'm just jealous."

"Of Sébastien?"

"Of anyone who can just simply spend some time with you," he says with a sudden sadness in his voice. "Of everyone alive."

I snuggle up against him. "I'm so sorry."

"Hey, we don't apologise for me being dead, remember."

His answer brings a small smile to my face "No, we don't. But we can still agree that it sucks."

"Oh yeah. It sucks majorly."

CHAPTER 10

The next day, I finally follow up on Jacques de Molay's request and approach Victor in the crypt. He listens to my proposal with a stern expression on his face, his eyebrows sinking deeper and deeper the more I explain. "So, all he wants is to meet you and have a chat, I suppose."

The Panthéon is already closed, so I don't have to worry about being out of place. Victor takes a full minute of silent contemplation before he grumbles. "No."

"What do you mean no?" I don't understand what's wrong with a simple conversation.

"The answer is no. He must not enter the crypt."

It takes all my strength not to roll my eyes. "Not even for a quick chat? You could meet him outside, you know."

"But he didn't ask for that, did he?" He makes it sound so mysterious, like it's an important distinction.

"What is it about this place?"

"It's sacred to the Great People of France."

Hard eye-roll this time. "It wouldn't hurt you to be a little more open. You took Gaspar in and you're still… fine."

Victor narrows his eyes again. "That remains to be seen."

So, Gaspar is still on probation. I'm disappointed. I expected more from the "Great People of France."

"Anyway, he doesn't belong here. So, no, I will not grant him an audience," Victor insists.

I'm not ready to give up so easily, because I'm the one who will have to deal with Molay's disappointment. "Does he truly not belong? Or is it just a formality. I would argue that the last Grand Master of the Knights Templar is one of the greats."

Victor scoffs. "For what? Devil worship? Being burned at the stake? Now, if you'd get your hands on Jeanne d'Arc, we might talk, but Jacques de Molay? How much veneration does he need? He already has a place on the Île de la Cité. The only reason anyone talks about him at all is because of all the stupid films and games your generation produces."

"How many films and games have they made of you?" I'm not much of a gamer, but I highly doubt there's a game in the works featuring Victor Hugo.

I've hurt his pride. Victor pulls himself upright, his pot belly protruding slightly as he straightens his coat. "I prefer to live through my works than through my person."

"That wasn't the case when you got involved in politics."

"Anyone who is someone has to get involved in politics. And not in the way Molay did."

"He didn't even do anything. You don't really think he was a devil worshipper." I've brushed up on Molay's history and it's clear to me that these were lies created by the king to gain control of the little city-state the Templars had built, and the treasures they had amassed by protecting pilgrims on their way to the Holy Land during the time of the Crusades. A smear campaign using the crude means of the time.

Victor shrugs. "Who knows? They were dark times indeed. Still, if any Templar deserves a place here, it should be Hugues de Payens, the humble knight who created the Order, not the proud Grand Master who saw it crumble."

"We'll have to agree to disagree on that, because the historical sources very clearly suggest that the Templars were framed for Philip's benefit."

"Do the sources suggest that or is that what *modern* historians with their *modern* sensibilities have decided?"

I feel oddly insulted that he would so disregard my profession, but I suppose I shouldn't be surprised, seeing how he feels about himself and everyone else who isn't part of that illustrious little circle.

"Very little of what was laid at Molay's feet had any merit. The Templars were good men. What they confessed under isolation, manipulation, and torture is baseless."

Victor crosses his arms. "The answer remains no, Alix. I will not budge from it."

"Not even for me?"

"I've already taken in your little ghost boyfriend, but he's harmless. He'll be gone in a century or less, never holding any kind of sway. Ghosts like Molay, who have been around for almost a millennium are of a different calibre. They have power."

I have to breathe through his words, for his dismissal of Gaspar hurts me physically. A hundred years is a long time—I'll be dead myself by then—but there's this sudden sense of mortality attached to him, as if he could die on me again.

Pushing those thoughts away, I try to concentrate on what he said about Molay. "What kind of power?"

"Didn't you feel it when you visited him? They say he cursed the king and the pope to die—"

"Rewritten history. Contemporary sources made no mention of the curse. It only became a legend because of the timing of their deaths, not before. It's like making a prophecy after the fact."

Victor grits his teeth in frustration. "That may be, but from the rumours I have heard, spending any amount of time near his bones has severe effects on your mental health."

This time I keep my mouth shut. Victor is right this time. Jacques de Molay's Nexus group has its headquarters in the Boutique of Psychosis. I felt the effects myself, but I thought it was the room that was to blame, not Molay himself. I'm still not sure if he is, or if this is all part of the urban legend that has only grown since his death.

"I think you're being stubborn."

"And I think you're being audacious." He sighs, his face softening again. "You're currently having a rough time, kid. But getting mixed up with the ghosts of the catacombs is not the way to go. Be careful."

I refrain from pointing out that Molay won't let me out of the deal, but then I sneer at my own silliness. I'll just have to explain to him how I tried, and then I can let the whole thing go. It looks like I won't be able to complete my last favour.

Still frustrated, I leave Victor alone and meet Gaspar at the top of the stairs. "Did you hear that?"

"That I'm an insignificant blot on the great fabric of human life? Yeah."

"I'm sorry." That was really harsh, whether it's true or not.

Gaspar shrugs. "Don't be. You said it yourself. I never had the chance to be more than I already am. And what I am—or was—isn't much."

"Well, if it helps, you're everything to me."

A smile appears on his face. "Yes, yes, that helps a lot. I'll be anything for you."

I'm well aware I shouldn't bind myself so tightly to his soul, but I can't seem to help it. As long as I don't *act* on my feelings, I should be fine. At least that's what I tell myself. "I need some fresh air," I tell him, packing up and leaving the Panthéon and its ridiculous ghost politics behind.

Outside, the air smells of rain. It's already dark, and the street lamps cast their amber light over glistening cobblestones. Gaspar accompanies me, probably not too keen on hanging around ghosts who only see him as a sort of pet.

"I can't believe that Victor and Voltaire—especially Voltaire, being a child of the Age of Reason—are so prejudiced against Molay."

Gaspar gives me a sheepish shrug. "Honestly, I don't even know who this Molay guy is. I thought the Knights Templars were just some myth."

"Oh no, they're real, even if their legendary treasures and all that is pure fiction. I mean, don't get me wrong, they were rich, but there's no hidden treasure chamber under Paris." At least I can't believe it hasn't been found after all this time and all this public interest.

"Damn. That would have been cool, though." Gaspar chuckles, then nudges me. "Come on, don't tell me you never wanted to be like Indiana Jones, digging up ancient treasures from hidden temples... or deep in the catacombs."

I can't help laughing because it's such a cliché. "How old do you think I am? Indiana Jones are dad movies."

Gaspar scoffs. "The audacity!"

Leave it to him to make me laugh when I'm in such a bad mood. "I love history because of all the cool facts, how they weave together and create this picture of the past. And my biggest dream wouldn't be to find some treasure, but to find a historical artefact that rewrites history. You know if we're being ridiculous here." I know very well that most of the sources have been examined over and over again, and unless I find a real historical treasure, my contributions to the field will involve obscure details that no one but my peers will ooh and aah over.

"What about bones?" Gaspar asks innocently.

"What about—?" Lightning strikes me. *What about bones? What about Molay's bones?* "Wait, are you thinking what I'm thinking?"

"Nobody else knows it's Molay buried down there, right?" Gaspar asks, now all serious. "But I guess you can't prove it."

I shake my head, my mind already racing through the possibilities. "Oh, there are ways nowadays." The idea manifests itself and

I find myself unable to let it go. In fact, it fills me with exhilaration. "Let's get Molay here."

By now I've learned that I can somehow will ghosts to come to me. Molay appears mere seconds after I have deliberately thought of him, his imposing figure appearing on the steps below us. As before, he's wearing his white cloak and chain mail armour. He has such a presence that I get a bit tongue-tied when his eyes meet mine.

"Have they agreed to see me?" his deep, rumbling voice cuts through my nerves.

"No..." My voice is much lower than it should be. Annoyed, I clear my throat, but before I can elaborate, Molay's face darkens.

"No?" His voice is like thunder now. "They said no? How dare they? What did they die for? How many thousands of people did they save with their pens and books?"

I swallow hard. This isn't exactly how I planned for this to go. "Not all of them were writers and philosophers," I mumble. Personally, I don't think military distinction should be the only way into the Panthéon, but it's not like there aren't any soldiers. "Most of the people interred initially were generals and other decorated soldiers from the Napoleonic Wars, such as Jean Lannes de Montebello or Michel Ordener."

Molay snorts at me. "And you think these so-called generals deserve their place? Above me? There are ghosts in there that even *you* would find it hard time to remember a single noteworthy thing about their lives. Surely, I deserve at least an *audience*." He says the last word in utter disgust, clearly considering himself above a common supplicant.

"You deserve more than that."

"Yes." Not a shred of doubt in sight. His piercing gaze lands on me. "I trust our deal still stands."

I begin to realise this isn't a typical favour. I won't be able to back out of it. Fortunately, I've got a plan to make it happen. "Of course it does. I just need you to have some patience."

Molay has regained his composure and gives me a sharp nod. "Good."

He turns around, but suddenly I have another question. If I'm going to go to all this trouble, I need to know more. "Grand Master." How strange to address someone like that. When he raises an eyebrow, I hurry to continue. "Why is this conversation so important to you?"

Instead of answering, Molay climbs the stairs until he towers over me. "Because, for better or worse, the Panthéon ghosts hold our fate in their hands. They've been chosen as the most capable people in all of France. Their word has power. And the ghosts need power, otherwise our existence remains fruitless."

I realise I've been holding my breath. "What exactly are you planning?" I whisper.

He sighs. "Structure, purpose." Shaking his head, he glances forlornly at the Panthéon. "They don't understand what it's like to be cast into the shadows, your name reduced to a whisper in the wind. When no one remembers who you really were but makes up bigger and wilder stories that still pale in front of the truth. We live a pitiful existence, and for what purpose? To be remembered? I saved thousands of lives in the short time I was alive. Now I have nothing."

As moving as his speech is, it leaves me even more confused. "And what will you gain from the Panthéon's support?"

His face softens. "Legitimacy. My living days are long gone, but my dead days will continue for the foreseeable future. There's change afoot. The dead are turning their backs on the living. There's only so long one can happily watch others grow and evolve. I dream of creating a commune—not unlike the Marais in my lifetime—a purpose for ghosts, structure, stability, a community far removed from the needs the living. But to bring us all together, I need the power of the Panthéon."

Stunned, I can only stare at him. Instead, Gaspar steps forward. "I'd love to pick your brain about this sometime." He sounds completely in awe. It's probably a sociologist's dream scenario.

Molay gives him a pitiful look. "Don't take this the wrong way, but you've only been dead for a mere second. Maybe in a few years, when you truly understand what it means to be a ghost in this world." And with that, he leaves us.

I step forward to rub Gaspar's arm, feeling infinitely sorry for him. He's so ready to find some meaning again, but maybe Molay is right. Gaspar hasn't even fully processed his death, let alone mourned his life. "You'll be surprised how quickly time passes."

He gives me a weary smile. "Yeah, and then I'll be gone. For real this time."

"Oh, Gaspar."

With a sudden shake of his head, he pulls himself together. "Who needs old Templars or famous writers? Most of us never change the world in any significant way. We just live our lives. So, I'll just live my death. Attend a few free concerts, continue classes, and help you."

I smile at him. "You're definitely welcome to stay as long as you like." If it helps him find his feet, I'm happy to keep him company.

CHAPTER 11

That night, I take Gaspar to Gaby to get her to help me with this crazy new idea. I don't yet know if I can pull this off, but I'm excited just thinking about it. We all dream of changing the world—in the small ways we can—and this could be my chance.

"You want to officially rediscover Jacques de Molay's bones and then lobby for them to be placed in the Panthéon?" Gaby asks, her eyes wide.

"Stupid idea?" I ask, worried that it has really got away from me.

Gaby sputters. "No, it could actually work. Theoretically, at least. I mean, what do we need? The bones, obviously."

I've already thought about it, so I list, "A series of links that plausibly lead to the *discovery*. Evidence. We should read up on DNA testing to support the claim."

"It would be nice to have Molay's testimony," Gaspar muses.

"Yes, that would be nice."

"What? DNA testing?" Gaby asks.

"Oh no, to have Molay's testimony. Gaspar just..." I take a deep breath. "He's here right now."

Gaby's eyes widen slightly, and I can see her struggling to keep her composure. "I thought you guys broke up," she whispers, as if that makes a difference.

"Do you want me to go?" Gaspar asks.

"No." I click my tongue, annoyed at how this answer confuses Gaby even more. I turn to her. "Yes, we broke up, and we're still broken up, but he decided to help me, as a friend."

Gaby gets to her feet. "I need wine for this."

"Do you want him to leave?" I don't want Gaspar to leave, since this was as much his idea as it was mine. Plus, he might be important to the plan.

Gaby pours us both some wine—she's that nice. "No, I mean, it's just a bit strange." She takes a sip from her glass. "He's going to leave with you, right? No offence," she says to the air next to her.

"Why wouldn't I?" Gaspar looks confused.

I, on the other hand, understand my friend. "Yes, of course he's going to leave. He's not a peeping Tom."

"Of course I'm not!"

While Gaspar is outraged, Gaby takes a big gulp of wine. "Good." Then she wrinkles her nose. "Now that you mention it. There could be a ghost watching me all the time." She shudders.

"Just think about it. All the creeps and perverts who can now spy on girls to their hearts' content."

"There's never been a ghost in your apartment. At least not while I've been here."

Gaby waves me off. "Go on. We have important business to discuss." She pulls out the board from under her bed, the one we made last time. Jacques de Molay is right there under Nexus. Gaby taps on his name. "So, he'll be your last favour, right?" She doesn't have to sound so relieved.

"Yes, Hélène's dream will finally come true. I will give up ghosts. Present company excluded."

Gaspar smiles smugly, causing me to jab my elbow into his side. "Just don't ask me for any favours."

Once again, I catch Gaby staring. This is obviously testing the boundaries of our friendship. Not wanting to lose her—especially for a boy I've only just met—I scoot closer and give her a quick hug. "Sorry."

She shakes her head, forcing a smile. "No, don't be. I know how much he meant to you. I'm sorry the two of you don't get to be a cute couple. You deserve it."

"Agreed." Gaspar crosses his arms, scowling as he nods.

I shrug and take a sip from my own glass. "I'm not meant for that."

"Rubbish!" Gaby immediately takes offence on my behalf. "You will absolutely have a normal, sweet relationship. You know, you're always so worried about how any potential partner will react to the ghosts, as if you have to marry the first person you get serious with. How about some casual sex like any normal twenty-something?"

My cheeks grow incredibly hot, and I keep glancing at Gaspar.

Gaby immediately notices my reaction. "Right. Um, sorry. Sorry, Gaspar." This time the direction of her gaze is almost right. "No sex talk tonight." She snorts. "That being said, it's been way too long for me, so maybe I'm projecting a bit. Because—"

"Jacques de Molay," I hasten to say.

"Him?" She catches herself and laughs. "Right, Molay's favour. Um, there's obviously two parts to the plan here. One, we need to find his bones and make sure they're correctly identified as those of Jacques de Molay. I'll look into how that usually works. And most importantly, how long it will take."

She hands me her glass and scribbles some more notes on the board. Gaspar is also leaning over the board, curiously reading our notes on Nexus, the Chevalier, and GoPol, while I wait patiently for Gaby to continue.

At last, she puts down her pen. "Secondly, we have to campaign for his inclusion in the Panthéon. That will also take time, but I guess we can do it simultaneously."

I'm beginning to realise this plan of mine isn't exactly a sure thing. We'll have to face a lot of sceptics, convince people to invest in it, and then convince them that he deserves to be interred in the Panthéon. After Victor's protest, I'm afraid the living side of things will have similar reservations.

"Our safest bet is to make this as public as possible. The discovery of Jacques de Molay's bones can't just be a footnote in the news of historical research, it has to attract national attention."

For some reason, Gaby starts to grin at me, her thoughts a mile ahead. "And who better to do that than you?"

"Um, what?" I'm not sure I can follow her. A weird thought crosses my mind. "You're not talking about using Malou's social media reach for this?"

Gaby starts to laugh, almost splashing wine all over her sheets. "As adorable and popular as your little hedgehog is, I don't think her target audience is the kind of attention we need. No, I'm talking about a more serious media outlet. You need to get your father on board."

"What does your father do?" Gaspar asks.

"He's an investigative journalist. His pieces are often published in *Le Monde* and other newspapers."

"Yes," says Gaby, slightly irritated. "That's why... Oh, you explained that to Gaspar."

Immediately, I turn back to her. "Yes, sorry. Um, you know what, that's actually not a bad idea." The more I think about it, the more I think it's a great idea. "Maman mentioned that he was a cataphile in his youth. So he'd probably be up for a trip down there. And he's finished his piece on the government sex scandals, so he's probably looking for a new project."

"Perfect!" I love that Gaby is as excited as me now. Are you going to tell him about the ghosts?"

"No!" Just the thought of it makes me cringe. "He'll never take me seriously if I do. No, no, I'll tell him about the Boutique and what I found there, and why I think it's Molay."

Gaby nods thoughtfully. "And then while you're down there, you whet his appetite with all the juicy historical details that show what an important French figure he is."

I have to laugh a little, imagining how Gaby thinks I could manipulate my father. I might as well tell him to include the bid for the Panthéon in his article. It would have the same chance of success. "He's a professional, Gaby. He'll do his own research on Molay and probably write a very objective series of articles about him."

Gaby begins to pout. "Oh, but it can't be dry as a bone." Once again, she looks roughly in Gaspar's direction. "Sorry for that turn of phrase."

"I don't think my bones are dry yet," he deadpans.

Chuckling, I put down my wine glass and write the second part of our plan on the board. Then I start to make action points. "We need to become experts on Molay if we want any chance of being involved in the official discovery. Maybe talk to the department, get some professors on board so it's not taken out of our hands right away. The most important thing is to establish a link on how he ended up in the Boutique." A thought crosses my mind and I shrug. "I guess I could ask him when Papa and I go down to the catacombs."

"You really want to go down there again?" Gaspar asks suddenly, looking incredibly worried. "Alone?"

My enthusiasm slightly dampened, I say, "I wouldn't be alone."

"The Chevalier is still down there."

I sigh. In all the excitement of making a plan, I haven't considered my recent terrifying experiences. "Maybe it's like riding a horse. You have to get back up..."

Gaspar's scowl deepens. "This isn't about breaking a bone."

"What's going on?" Gaby whispers.

"Gaspar is worried I'll run into the Chevalier down there."

Great! Now Gaby looks scared too. "Maybe it's not such a good idea after all."

"I could ask Sébastien if he'd like come along."

"Oh, is he Sébastien now?" Gaby widens her eyes for effect.

I wave her off. "Well, we'll be related someday, so..." I remember that I haven't told her about my latest revelation. "Actually, there's something important I have to tell you. Sébastien told me why I'm a ghost whisperer."

My teaser is met with great confusion. "There's a reason?"

"Yes, apparently ghost whisperers like him and me are the way we are because we've all had near-death experiences. The real kind, where they had to bring you back from the brink."

Confusion turns to concern. "You never told me about that."

"That's because I can't remember. Apparently, when that happens, a ghost of you is created, and that creates the connection to the ghost world. Sébastien died—so to speak—when he was seventeen. He's got his seventeen-year-old ghost, Dix... Sept," I add to avoid confusion, "with him all the time. Dix spies for him, guards his back and is basically an extension of him. It's different with me. Since I can't remember when I had such an accident, Sébastien believes my ghost was formed when I was very small, which would be much less helpful."

I shudder at the thought of having to convince a toddler to help me.

Gaby has become incredibly quiet. She takes sip after sip from her wine glass, staring at me with her eyes wide open. Her voice quavers as she asks, "This is real. Like really, really real?"

This must all sound incredibly crazy. "I've met Dix. He's a ghost. And he truly does look like a younger Sébastien."

She takes a deep breath, closing her eyes. "Alright. I have to remember that a proper policeman told you all this."

"I'm putting a lot on you tonight, aren't I?" Full of pity, I rub her back.

Gaby smiles weakly at me. "A lot, but never too much. I just need a moment to wrap my head around it and readjust my view of the world." She suddenly frowns. "But if that's true, shouldn't there be a lot more ghost whisperers?"

The thought hadn't occurred to me yet. "Probably. But we already know that there are others like me."

Unconvinced, Gaby wrinkles her nose. "They should be much more common." She gives up easily, though. "But back to our plan. You want to involve Sébastien?"

"He seems like a logical choice, and he was keen on helping me."

"With ghost favours?" Gaby asks doubtfully.

I shrug. "I don't see why not. Having him and Dix with us would definitely make me feel safer."

"What about me?" Gaspar asks suddenly.

I look at him and notice he's still frowning. "What about you?"

"You know, I can do what Dix does," he says hastily, almost stumbling over his words. "If Sébastien's right, and your ghost is practically a baby, you'll need your own useful companion. I could be that."

"What exactly are you suggesting?" I'm not quite sure I'm ready to have Gaspar around indefinitely. As much as I'd like to be with him, his constant presence would certainly ensure I'd never be able to move on. Maybe that's exactly what he wants. Can I really blame him for holding on to me?

Next to me, Gaby mutters, "This is really weird."

"Sorry," I whisper back, feeling the guilt of doing this to her grow.

Gaspar looks at his hands before making a decision. "I can be useful. If you insist on going back to the catacombs, whether with him or just your father, I can make sure you're safe."

"How?"

"By spying on le Chevalier d'Os. He runs his operations from the Crossroad of the Dead, right? I can go there, eavesdrop, and at least find out what he's planning, whether it's safe to enter the catacombs or not. That would be helpful, wouldn't it?" His question betrays his desperation. He needs this as much as I do.

"Will you be safe?"

"I'm dead, Alix," Gaspar says a little more forcefully than he probably intended.

I swallow. "He had a ghost whisperer at his disposal."

"Yeah, but there are hundreds of ghosts at the Crossroad, and she won't *always* be with him. I'll make sure I stay out of sight when she's around." His eyes turn pleading. "Please, Alix. Please let me do this for you. I want to help."

Finally, I pull myself together. "Alright." Turning to Gaby, I explain, "Gaspar will spy on the Chevalier for me and make sure it's safe to go in with my papa. As long as we avoid the Crossroad of the Dead, we should be fine. When Emily and I went to the Boutique, no one bothered us."

She nods, accepting my course of action without further protests. "Okay, Gaspar will take care of that, and you and I will start researching Molay."

I smile at her. "Perfect."

CHAPTER 12

V isiting Square du Vert-Galant in late autumn is not a lot of fun. What is a verdant green tip of Île de la Cité in summer is now a dull, cold, and very wet place. The grey waves of the Seine splash against the already rain-soaked banks. There are no people lounging on the grass, just a few souls resilient enough to brave the weather for a quick stroll and view from the tip. Not that there's much to see with the clouds hanging low.

Somewhere a child is crying, the only sound in the pitter-patter of the rain. Gaby pulls her coat tighter and fights with her umbrella. "Not much to see here, is there?" Her voice is tinges with hope. She probably can't wait for us to turn in.

"I suppose not."

Seven hundred years ago, on the 18th March 1314, Jacques de Molay was executed on this square, burned at the stake. It would have been a huge spectacle, the mighty Grand Master of the Knights Templar brought to his knees. He would have been an old man, stout and proud, but unable to turn the tide in the face of a series of false testimonies and a king's thirst for blood—and money.

There is little information to be gained about what happened here. At the entrance to the square there is a large sign summarising its history and there's a plaque commemorating Jacques de Molay where he was burned alive. The sign is a bit lacking in detail, and the plaque is just that. Neither captures the horrors of the time nor the day of his death, let alone the intricacies surrounding it.

"Is he here?" Gaby whispers.

"Molay?" He should be. This is the only place in Paris where he is remembered. There is no official burial place, no tomb to visit. His ties to the living world are strongest here. And yet there's no sign of him. I could probably summon him if I needed to, but he's probably staying away from the place where he met his end for a reason. Summoning him would be a jerk move.

I shake my head. "No. And I don't think we'll find any trace of him here." I had hoped there would be some clue as to what happened to his remains. Of course, I know where they are, but not how they got there, which is important if I want to make a case that will stand up in the scientific community.

"Let's go to the Marais and find a nice café to warm up before we take a stroll through his old neighbourhood." Gaby struggles a little more with her umbrella before managing to turn around and head back across the island towards the twin towers of Notre Dame.

We cross the Pont d'Arcole to the mainland and land right on the corner of the Marais. Before the Templars got hold of the land, it was just a boring stretch of marshland, hence the name. The Templars drained the land and made it fertile before building their huge fortress in the north of the district. Like so many historic buildings, the fortress has been completely demolished. Only its gates have survived, not in situ, but in one of the many museums scattered around the Marais.

Back then, there would have been cobbled streets, white-robed Templars, and groups of pilgrims. Today the district is home to chic boutiques, galleries, and gay bars. It's the place to be, and even Victor Hugo had a chic apartment on the Place des Vosges, which has been turned into yet another museum—not that he spends much time there these days. The only traces of the Templars are a street, a square, and a Métro station named after them.

Gaby and I find a fancy pâtisserie near the Square du Temple where we order coffee and two slices of different gateaux, which we promptly split between the two of us. With sugar pumping through our veins and the warm heater of the pâtisserie, we soon feel a lot better about ourselves.

Like the Île de la Cité, the Templar Square is a beautiful green oasis in the warmer months of the year. It's still pretty now, although the trees are bare, and the grass has been washed away.

"So, what's the deal with you and Gaspar?" Gaby says carefully as she digs her fork into her cake.

I'm surprised she's only bringing it up now, but not that it's happening. As usual, my best friend is looking out for me. "I told you: we broke up."

She winces. "You said that. But he's still following you around. Is *he* here?"

"No. He's probably down in the catacombs as promised." I sigh, not really keen on getting into this. "I think he struggles a lot with … well, with his accident." I deliberately avoid the word death, so as not to draw attention to ourselves. Despite the bad weather, the cafés and restaurants in the Marais are full.

"Understandable."

"Yes. And he's been told he doesn't belong in either community. He's not famous enough for the Panthéon and not experienced enough for Nexus, despite his cataphilic ways." Belatedly, I add, "And he doesn't belong with me either." Now that I've put it into words, I feel even more sorry for him. "I think he feels adrift. Caught between worlds. A bit like me."

Gaby reaches across the table and squeezes my hand. "You're still here. Life has so much to offer you. You just have to grab it and hold on to it."

I smile at her, trying to ease her worries. I know life is wonderful, but it's never going to get easier. Even though I've distanced myself from Gaspar, there are still so many other ghosts I know and love.

"Yes, but what I mean is he's just trying to find a place for himself. It's a huge adjustment."

"A place by your side?" Gaby asks doubtfully.

"Only for now," I hasten to say, because that would be sensible. Sensible and expected.

Gaby seems satisfied with my answer. "You know what's best for you."

I doubt it very much, but we'll go with it. As I finish my cake, I let my gaze wander over the square and try to imagine what life would have been like in the medieval fortress. Would the Templars have trained in the rain, or would they have huddled around the fire inside, telling each other stories of the Holy Land? Would they have written letters to their loved ones, like Abelard and Héloïse?

All these lives and possible futures. For two hundred years, they've had such a huge impact on France and the European landscape around the Crusades. And then it all came to a sudden and violent end.

Claims of devil worship, blasphemy, and of course, the always-cited homosexuality were lain at their feet, basically the trifecta of medieval accusations. At first, the people were on their side. Even the pope couldn't believe they had suddenly gone from holy warriors to sinners. But lies and false confessions built the case. Details were "accidentally" leaked as gossip, and soon everyone cheered as they burned the alleged heretics at the stake.

Something catches my eye. A white banner with a red cross, the symbol of the Templars. Is it a ghost vision? Is there even such a thing? No, there really is a Templar banner hanging from a window across the square.

"Hey Gaby. Let's check this out" I get up from of my chair and quickly finish my cup of coffee.

Gaby is already done. "Check out what?"

"Just come with me." We leave the pâtisserie in a hurry and cross the square. "Do you see that?"

I point ahead, where the banner is clinging to the wall. To my relief, Gaby sees it too, her eyes widening as she nods. "Yes. Is it a museum, perhaps?"

It isn't. Instead, it looks like a small church. We arrive at its doorstep and look for a sign that might indicate the opening hours. When we don't find one, I bravely try the handle. The door swings open, revealing nothing but a stone floor and darkness.

"Excuse me?" Gaby calls inside.

There are footsteps on the other side, and I jump back quickly, as if it changes the fact that I opened the door in the first place. A man opens the door all the way. He's about fifty years old with thin blonde hair that's receded so far on either side that there's a small island of tuft in the middle. Despite our trespass, he's got a friendly smile for us.

"How can I help you?"

I'm too nervous to answer, but Gaby has always been the more outgoing of the two of us. "Hello, I'm Gabrielle Lemel, and this is Alix Dubois. We're history students at the Sorbonne and we saw the Templar banner outside your church."

The smile deepens. "Ah, I think you're a little mistaken. It's not a Templar banner, but it's a common mistake." How embarrassing, having just declared ourselves history students. "It's the Order of Malta. Our history is intertwined with that of the Templars. But while our Order survived the centuries, the Templars did not."

"Yeah, that's why we're here. We're trying to find out more about the demise of the Templars. You wouldn't have some old texts or something like that?" I ask, slowly finding my stride.

"I might have something. Come on in. I'm Paul Laugier, the local priest." He glances at the rain. "It's terrible out there. I'll make some coffee."

Gaby and I follow him inside. As the heavy door closes behind us, I can't help but wonder what secrets we might discover here.

CHAPTER 13

I t turns out that the Order of Malta was a rival order to the Templars who largely despised the Templars' enterprising ways. Both served pilgrims, but only one of them survived the Crusades with its reputation intact.

"The Knights Hospitallers, as we call ourselves, were bound by three vows of poverty, chastity, and obedience," the priest explains over a cup of coffee. "Some of us still uphold those values—at least the first two," he adds with a chuckle. "They didn't take exorbitant fees from the pilgrims like the Templars but since they both had a similar role, there were a lot of clashes. In the end, when the Templars' reign came to an end, the Maltesers took in many of their knights, because in the end they had the same goals and ideals."

I perk up when I hear that. If the Maltesers were kind enough to take in their rivals to protect them from unjust persecution, they might have been kind enough to give Molay a proper burial after his execution.

"This may sound a bit far-fetched, but you don't happen to know what happened to the remains of the Templars? We've been looking for their graves." Not sure if the explanation makes it better, but I have to try.

Paul frowns as he tries to remember. "You don't mean the ones they burned, do you? Because…"

"Oh, burning at the stake isn't quite the same as cremation," Gaby chimes in. "Usually, you get charred bones left over when the fire burns down." A morbid but interesting fact.

Paul's eyes widen in surprise. "I see. Um, in that case… well, surely, you've heard about all those skeletons they unearthed at the Carreau du Temple in 2007." He squints at us. "Although, you might have been a bit young for that."

It's a bit embarrassing that we call ourselves history students and don't know that, but then again, most of our lessons have been about with events that happened at least fifty years ago. "Tell us more."

"Wait a minute." He stands and leaves the room.

"How did we not know that the Maltesers were a knightly order?" Gaby asks. She's got her phone out and is typing away furiously. A second later, I can hear her gasp. "This is surreal."

"What?"

She shows me her internet search and points to a word. "They are a sovereign state led by a prince," she exclaims. "And here I thought it was just doctors, nurses, and relief workers."

From what I can see in the excerpt on the phone, humanitarian aid is their main role these days, but they are a military order legitimised by the Pope, with a rather old-fashioned, aristocratic leadership system. Not exactly what I expected in the 21st century. Then again, I live in a country that's highly allergic to any form of nobility.

Before I can discuss the matter further with Gaby, Paul returns with a pile of newspapers, magazines, and old photographs. "I kept these because it happened just across the street." He puts them on the small table between us. "They were doing renovations, trying to restore the old building when they discovered a Templar cemetery underneath. They had to remove hundreds of skeletons before they could continue the work."

Intrigued, I pick up the documents he brought with him. The photos aren't very spectacular, just the Carreau in a scaffold and workers going in and out. Of course, no one let him take pictures of the skeletons they had dug up. The newspaper clippings are a bit more forthcoming. Apparently, they let journalists in—or at least released some pictures to the press. The headlines are the usual sensationalist crap. You'd think they'd found a zombie enclosure, instead.

I search the articles for any mention of Molay, but if there was any identification, it was after the press had already forgotten about the event. The lone magazine seems to be the only useful one, published in 2009, two years later. Its title is, 'Unearthing the Secrets of the Knights Templar', and it is at least forty pages thick with huge colour pictures and long articles.

"Could I borrow this, perhaps?"

Paul scratches the back of his head. "I'm quite fond of it. You know, I was interviewed for it about the history of the Maltesers." He smiles, proud as a child. "My only claim to fame."

"I'll bring it back for sure. Or if you'd rather I took pictures of the pages?"

"Nah, it's fine. You can borrow it. Maybe bring it back in a week and leave me your phone number and address." With that, the matter seems to be settled. With an expectant look at us, he clasps his hand. "So, what is this for, if I may ask? A class assignment?"

Gaby laughs. "More like us going down the rabbit hole. We're trying to find out where the remains of Jacques de Molay are buried."

A sharp wrinkle appears on the priest's forehead. "Okay?" He sounds confused.

"You know, in all the history books and accounts online, his story always ends with the execution," Gaby explains, doing an amazing job of making us seem fairly normal—by history student standards, anyway. "I mean, there's always some bit about his legacy, like how he cursed the king and the pope with his dying breath."

Paul has become surprisingly quiet. He seems completely engrossed in Gaby's story, but also growing more sceptical by the minute. Maybe she's not doing such a good job, after all.

I jump in to help her. "We know that's nonsense, of course. Historical research suggests that the curse was added in later years because the two men who betrayed him died within a year."

"Sounds more like divine intervention to me," Paul mutters.

Not wanting to argue about God with a religious man, I just nod. "That's as likely as a curse."

"The curse just fits in better with his whole devil worship thing," Gaby jokes.

Instead of laughing, Paul's frown deepens. "I heard about that."

"It was just a lie," I can't help saying.

"A lie?" Paul seems a little lost.

"Well, it's the kind of accusation that was thrown around a lot back then. And in retrospect, it seems clear that King Philippe was determined to bring them down. Molay wasn't really a devil worshipper. There's no such thing as a devil, is there?"

Paul's reaction is a little delayed, but then he laughs. "Of course, of course. Those were all lies." I notice that he doesn't exactly rush to proclaim Molay's innocence either. Perhaps some of the old rivalry has been passed down despite the Malteser's aid to the persecuted Templars. "Would you like to see some paintings of how the temple used to look?"

Gaby and I exchange glances. "Sure."

Having regained his enthusiasm, Paul almost jumps out of his chair and leads us to a room at the back where a series of beautiful paintings depict medieval life around the temple. Until now I hadn't quite grasped how big the Templar fortress was. It was *massive*. Big enough to house thousands of knights, servants, and all the livestock they needed to support themselves. I can easily imagine it towering over the Marais, a safe haven—or so everyone thought.

"Uncle?" A light woman's voice echoes through the church. "Uncle, where are you hiding?"

"Back here, darling," Paul calls, then turns to us. "My niece is staying with me while she studies at the Sorbonne."

A moment later, a familiar face appears. It's Marie, Gaspar's colleague from the café. "There you are." She notices me almost immediately. "Alix? What are *you* doing here?"

"You two know each other?" Paul and Gaby ask almost simultaneously.

"Alix is one of my loyal customers at *Chambelland*." She smiles at me. "What brings you *here* of all places?"

I point at the pictures. "Knights Templar history. We're trying to find the remains of Jacques de Molay, the last Grand Master of the Order."

"Fun!" Marie exclaims, then seems to realise what she's said. "I mean... it sounds interesting."

Paul raises an eyebrow. "Interesting is one way to put it," he mutters.

"Um." Gaby clears her voice behind me, causing me to step aside.

"Oh, right. Marie, this is my best friend, Gabrielle. Gaby, Marie is one of Gaspar's colleagues." As soon as I add that, I have to swallow a little. One day it'll be easier to think about his death, I'm sure.

Marie seems to be delighted to make Gaby's acquaintance and immediately holds out her hand. "Did you know him too?"

Flustered, Gaby stares at the hand. "Um... no? No, not really." She finally shakes Marie's hand, then quickly hides it behind her back as if embarrassed.

I give her a confused look while Marie turns to her uncle. "I was going to cook dinner, but I noticed we're out of cream, so I'm going to pop out for a bit. Is there anything else we need?"

"No, I think I'm fine."

Marie gives us a friendly wave, which I catch Gaby mindlessly returning, and leaves. Paul smiles gently. "I'm glad she's feeling a bit better. I've missed her little whirlwind self."

"Better?" Gaby asks, and I almost want to nudge her with my elbow. She's not usually so slow.

"There was a tragedy at her café. Her co-worker had an accident." Paul frowns. "You know him," Paul suddenly accuses me.

"*Knew* him," I stress.

"Of course, of course." He nods with all the appropriate gravity.
"My condolences. Now, is there anything else I can help you with,
or are we done for today?"

We've probably imposed on him quite a bit, so I shake my head.
"We're good. I'll read the magazine and get it back to you as soon
as I can."

"Great. If you have any questions, I'll be happy to answer them
then. Good luck with your search."

The priest shows us the door, and to our delight the rain has
slowed to a drizzle. It's only when the door closes behind us that I
nudge Gaby. "You like her."

Her cheeks immediately blush. "You never told me how beautiful she was. Come to think of it, you never told me about *Chambelland*. It's a café near the university, isn't it? How often have you
been there?"

I didn't think Gaby would appreciate me haunting the places
Gaspar frequented. "A couple of times." I give in with a sigh.
"When Gaspar and I first met, he took me there. I like their coffee."

"Oh yes, the coffee," Gaby teases. "You don't go there for the
coffee at all."

"Well, looks to me like you'd like the coffee too."

Gaby laughs and links her arm in mine. "I have to at least try it!"

CHAPTER 14

As soon as I get back home, I dive straight into the magazine. It's incredibly interesting. I would probably find more detail in the articles published in professional historical journals—something I'll try later—but the articles in this one are much more engaging, written for public consumption.

There's a lot about the history of the Templars, and I find myself drawn into events that have nothing to do with Molay. But of course, Molay gets his own four-page feature. I've just started reading it when my mother asks me to help her in the kitchen. We're expecting Hélène and Cédric for dinner and my maman wants to serve her popular chicken chasseur. I'm in charge of the bread and onion soup for the starter. Later, there's also crème brûlée.

I take the opportunity to interrupt our idle chat with some research of my own. "So, Maman, I'm healthy, right?"

She gives me a perplexed look. "I hope so."

"I mean, I don't have any underlying conditions I should be aware of?"

"What's this about?" She still sounds amused. "Are you going to take up Cédric's offer and apply to the police?"

I'm confused for a minute until I realise that there's probably some sort of physical examination before you enter the police academy. "No, definitely not. Although I could join his cousin." The work of GoPol sounds much more interesting. A career in ghosts! Then again, I like history.

"His cousin?" Maman asks as she pours the white wine into the pan and the steam rises.

I pause chopping onions for a moment. "Oh, didn't he tell you about his cousin Sébastien? He's also a policeman, although he works for the secret service."

Maman is intrigued. "Really? That's interesting. I suppose Cédric isn't allowed to divulge many details. How do you know this cousin?"

"I joined Hélène and Cédric for lunch in town the other day. Sébastien was there too." I hide the fact that it was the other way round, neither planned nor welcome. Sébastien fled as soon as Cédric appeared.

"Are they trying to set you two up?" Maman asks amused. "That's nice, I suppose." She suddenly looks at me with concern.

I concentrate on the onions, which are starting to affect my eyes. As if I needed a reason to cry. "How is that nice?"

"Well, I guess they're trying to cheer you up after things didn't work out with the other boy. It was the first relationship you've had in a long time."

"Which is exactly why I don't want to jump to the next guy. And it definitely won't be Sébastien." I will not be drawn into their strange police dynasty.

Maman seems scandalised. "Why not? Is he bad-looking? Or a jerk?"

"Neither," I mutter, suddenly seeing Sébastien's image before my eyes. He's a bit too stiff, but I can't deny that he looks rather dashing in his uniform. Not like Cédric, who always looks like a puffer fish stuck in a police uniform. And he's been nothing but kind and considerate so far. He even offered his help to me several times. Still, just because a man isn't an ass and looks nice is not nearly enough reason to date him.

"So, do you like him?" My mother is enjoying this far too much. She probably can't wait to see two of her daughters married off. If Odile isn't careful, she'll be engaged before she graduates.

"Maman!" I throw the onions into the pot with much less care than usual. "I'm not interested in him. I'll probably never see him again."

"You'll see him at the wedding," Maman points out.

I roll my eyes at her. "Maybe." Judging by Sébastien's quick exit from the restaurant, he may end up skipping the wedding. "Can we get back to the subject?"

"We had a subject?"

"Yes, my health."

Maman laughs. "What's with this sudden obsession? Shouldn't you know whether you need to see a doctor or not?"

"I don't remember much from when I was little."

She frowns at me now. "When you were little?"

"Yeah, like I don't remember if I ever had a little accident or had to go to the hospital."

My mother turns down the heat on her chicken and covers it with a lid to let it simmer gently for a while. "I can't remember anything major. All little children have accidents, you know."

"But nothing serious?" A near-death experience would certainly be considered major. "Could I see my medical records?"

"Sure," she says, although she doesn't sound very happy about it. "If you need to. I'll have to dig them out, so remind me later."

The doorbell rings and I hear my father's feet in the hall. A moment later, the air is filled with Hélène's bright chatter. The window of opportunity to get more information from my mother has passed.

There's little room at the table for anything not related to the wedding until we get to the crème brûlée. While Hélène enjoys the dessert, I manage to get into the conversation. "Papa?"

He looks up expectantly. "Yes?"

"Maman told me you used to be a cataphile in your youth."

Hélène glares at me immediately, while Odile exclaims, "No way!"

Papa seems a little flustered. "I may have been down there a few times." He looks at Cédric. "I hope it's not an issue."

Officer Cédric just puts on his cheesy smile. "Not at all. Though, perhaps I should leave the room until Alix has said her piece." Since he doesn't move to follow up his words, I assume that was his version of a joke.

"What's your piece?" Papa asks, intrigued.

"Oh, well, I've been doing this assignment on Jacques de Molay, the last Grand Master of the Knights Templar. And it all leads back to the catacombs. There are so many Templar-related structures down there." Not that I've checked on my tiny map which parts are actually under the Marais. I wouldn't be surprised if the Boutique was, though. "Anyway, I found this room with a skeleton in it."

My mother winces at the mention. "Do you have to?"

I ignore her. "It's more complete than the others, and the bones are charred. Gaby and I have done some research and I think there's a good chance it could be the remains of Jacques de Molay."

Odile moans in true teenage fashion. "Ugh, I can't believe you'd go to the catacombs for history. It's so boring."

"It may surprise you, Odi, but I'm a *history* student."

"Ha ha."

My father puts a hand on her arm before she can bring us all down with her condescending opinions and asks me with a jerk of his chin, "That sounds pretty interesting. What do you want from me?"

"I was wondering if you'd like to come with me while I do some research down there. If it really is Molay..." I leave the sentence open so he can fill in the blanks himself.

His face lights up. "Are you offering me the scoop here?"

I grin at him. "Would you be interested?"

"Hell, yes." Papa looks at Cédric, who immediately raises his hands.

"Don't look at me," he says. "I haven't heard anything of interest. Have you, darling?" He turns to Hélène.

When Hélène sighs and shakes her head, he winks at me, which makes me shudder. I don't know whether to be glad he's not trying to stop us from going or freak out. I don't know what it is about him that makes him so damn disingenuous, but I can't bring myself to trust him.

I decide to ignore him and smile at my father. "Awesome. Let's make a plan."

Papa nods happily. "Absolutely. I'll have to see when I have time for it, though."

"Sure." So far, Gaby's and my plan seems to be working perfectly. Of course, all the media attention is useless if I can't prove it's Molay.

Before she leaves, Hélène corners me in my room. "This is a ghost thing, isn't it?" she hisses, agitated.

"What if it is?" There's no point denying it in front of her these days.

She closes the door behind her with an exasperated huff. "Gosh, Alix. Are you going to drag Papa into this now?"

"You make it sound like I'm going on a drug binge."

"Honestly, you sound like it."

I can't help but gasp. "You don't get it, do you?"

Hélène has crossed her arms. "Get what?"

"This is my life. The ghosts will never go away. But they could actually be useful for once." That's not really fair to the ghosts. They've been very helpful with a lot of things over the years. "Nobody knows history better than them. By helping Molay, I benefit as well. Imagine the headlines. You've always wanted me to succeed, haven't you?"

If Hélène feels a hint of sarcasm, she doesn't show it. But she's run out of arguments. "This is about your career?"

It never really was, but I can't deny how great it would be if I succeeded. "More about justice," I answer truthfully, before admitting, "but it would also do wonders for my prospects."

"I see." Though still unhappy, the prospect of being respected in my chosen field seems to soothe my sister somewhat. "You must still be careful. But I suppose Papa knows what he's doing."

"And I don't?"

Wisely, Hélène refuses to answer. "Be careful. You're..." She hesitates.

"I'm what?" Surely it's going to be something terrible again. If only I'd listened to my wise older sister, life wouldn't be so damn hard.

"Vulnerable," she says with sudden conviction.

Now she's lost me. "Vulnerable?"

"You just lost someone you really liked. The one who turned into a ghost?" Her voice is deceptively soft.

My heart flutters as I realise what she's talking about. "He was always a ghost," I whisper.

Hélène's eyes soften even more. "Yes, you said that. Still, it must be incredibly hard."

"I'm fine," I blurt, but the tremor in my voice betrays me.

Her eyes downcast, she says, "It would be natural to rush into things. To take unnecessary risks, to chase after big, distracting dreams..."

"What do you know about losing someone?" I ask.

Hurt, Hélène takes a deep breath. "I'm sorry. I know he was real for you."

I can't believe she still treats ghosts as if they were just a figment of my imagination. "He was a real person. You can look him up, find pictures, friends…"

"But you weren't one of them," Hélène argues, unaware that it feels like a slap in the face. She closes her eyes and breathes in deeply. "What I mean is, I understand you have feelings for him and that you experience this loss as if he'd really been ripped out of your life, but the truth is he was dead before you met him. So, he was never real."

There's no point arguing with her. My sister is a lost cause. She probably thinks the same of me, but I'm done trying. "Thank you, Léni. I appreciate your voice of reason at this difficult time."

She immediately grimaces and gives me a flat stare. "No, you don't."

"No, I don't, but thank you anyway. Now. I need to do some more research." To demonstrate my point, I pick up the magazine and pretend to read it.

Hélène clicks her tongue in annoyance and thankfully leaves me alone. I don't put the magazine down until she's gone, staring at the door in front of me.

Doubt nags at me. Is that why I'm trying so hard to help Molay? Because I'd rather bury myself in work than deal with the fact my boyfriend is dead? If so, it's working. I've finally stopped crying every half hour. Life goes on—and so does the afterlife. At least I'm doing something productive instead of wallowing on my pillow all day.

This favour for Jacques de Molay may be my last, but it'll be my biggest one yet.

Chapter 15

I'm not surprised when Gaby suggests that we both go to *Chambelland* after our morning lecture. It's obvious to me she has a huge crush on Marie. And while Gaby finds a reason to chat her up, I retreat to the back of the café with Gaspar, who has returned from his scouting mission.

"He's carrying on as usual," Gaspar reports. "Still has his meeting room at the Crossroad of the Dead."

"Who's he meeting with?" I whisper, hiding my mouth behind a menu card. It's not ideal, but the café is fairly empty, and Marie is quite distracted by Gaby.

"All sorts of people. I recognise some of them as fellow cataphiles. They usually tell him about new tunnels they've discovered. Looks to me like he's refining his maps. I tried to get a look at them, but he seems to sense the ghosts. Not like you, but maybe like Malou."

A giggle escapes my lips, which I quickly cover up with a cough. "What is he doing then?"

"Rolling up the map. He's not bringing out the sage," Gaspar jokes. "But as far as I can tell, he's looking for rooms of power."

"Rooms of power?" I'm happy to accept that ghosts exist, but what's this about mysterious power?

Gaspar shrugs. "Like the Boutique of Psychosis, I suppose. A few others have been mentioned. Um... Monastery of the Bees... no Bears. And the Medusa. Strange names, even by catacombs standards."

"Has he been to any of them?"

"He rarely moves. Most of the time he just lords over the Crossroad, meeting people. Like a spider in his web."

I shudder at the thought. Whatever the Chevalier is up to, I don't want to get sucked into it again. I just hope his web doesn't cover every inch of the catacombs. "Do you think he has a job?"

Gaspar shakes his head. "Not up here. I didn't see it, but I'm pretty sure he's dealing on the black market. He got a few deliveries, and things went out."

"Lovely."

I'm distracted by a text from Sébastien: *What's this about Molay?*

With a groan, I shove the phone back into my bag. "I should've known Cédric would immediately run to his cousin."

"What?" Gaspar asks, confused.

"Oh, I asked Papa to come with me to the catacombs at the family dinner yesterday. I probably should've done it somewhere more private because my sister had another fit. Cédric was joking, but it was obviously just a front to make me feel safe. There's no other reason why Sébastien would suddenly ask me about it."

"I see." Gaspar leans back, crosses his arms behind his head and looks around the café. "I miss working here."

Unable to help myself, I put a hand on his arm. At the moment, *Chambelland* is empty, except for Gaby, Marie, and me. And Gaspar, of course. While Gaby is still flirting with Marie, the barista keeps looking at me, then shakes her head.

I drop my hand and stare at the table instead. Still, I hear footsteps approaching soon after.

"Um, Alix," Gaby asks surprisingly cautiously. She's accompanied by Marie, who looks fascinated and confused at the same time. "Marie said she sometimes feels like there's a *presence*."

"Of Gaspar. In the shop," Marie adds hastily.

It doesn't help that Gaspar is grinning wildly. I manage not to glare at him and look up at Gaby instead. "And...?"

"Well, I told her—"

"You didn't."

"Not like that!" Gaby hurries to say, earning a confused look from Marie. "I just said that you've had similar experiences before."

Marie decides to skip the awkwardness and jumps into the chair opposite me, before grabbing my hands and looking far too excited. "I'm a big fan of the occult, and I believe that people leave some sort of shadow behind when they go. A benevolent presence, or sometimes not-so benevolent. But my talent in that regard is very negligible. I've always wanted to meet a real psychic."

"I'm not a psychic."

Gaby gives me a pleading look. "Alix, please."

I sigh, wondering how my talents got dragged into this scheme of hers to make Marie fall for her.

"Come on," Gaspar nudges me. "Marie is cool. She won't freak out or anything."

He sounds keen to talk to her too, and I suppose the least I owe my best friend, after supporting me through all this, is to play along. "Alright. I have a connection to the... supernatural." Is that what psychics say?

"Am I right that he's here?" Marie asks excitedly.

I take a deep breath and close my eyes, pretending to sense the room. "Yes. This place has a strong hold on him."

"I'm only here because of you," Gaspar jokes.

"Not helpful," I mutter, then force a smile for Marie. "There are a lot of presences here, but yes, I think Gaspar is one of them."

When her shoulders sag with relief, I start to feel bad. She smiles softly. "That's nice. Can you tell him I miss his stupid face at work?"

Gaspar has gone quiet, solemnity setting in.

"He can hear you," I say, this time without any pretence in my voice. "I come here often, because even though we never visited together, it reminds me of him. It's a part of him."

"It was really just a part-time job to make ends meet," Gaspar whispers, but he doesn't sound so sure anymore. I know he wants to hold my hand, but it's not possible.

Marie smiles, but there is a tear in her eye. "I understand. I've started wearing his apron at work, even though they're exactly the same."

"Tell her I miss working with her too. She was my favourite colleague," Gaspar says suddenly.

I sigh. How am I going to explain this? Then again, psychics rarely explain anything, they just make it sound ominous, and maybe by phrasing it in a certain way, I can help him too. "I have the feeling," I say aloud, "that Gaspar misses this place as much as you miss him. He seems reluctant to stay. I detect a hint of guilt, or perhaps regret."

"What are you doing?" Gaspar hisses.

Marie's eyes soften. "Oh, he's always welcome here. I would like to feel his presence more often. It gives me hope that he's not gone forever, just moved on to another phase of existence."

"I suppose I could stay," Gaspar says reluctantly. I've noticed that he often acts as if he didn't have a life before. Seeing how much he's struggling to find his place in the afterlife, I'm beginning to think he needs to connect with his old life first.

"Please," I whisper. I blink and look up at Gaby. "It's time to go back, isn't it?"

"Is it?" Her mouth forms a small 'O'. "Yes. I had to check something at the library." She turns to Marie. "See you later?"

Marie smiles at her. "Yes. You're always welcome here."

As I stand up, I manage to run my fingers over Gaspar's leg to comfort him. Then we leave the two of them alone. Marie returns to her place behind the counter, while Gaspar hangs around the other side, watching her do the job he did just a few weeks before.

"What happened?" Gaby asks me as we leave the café.

"Nothing. I just noticed something. You know how Gaspar always hangs around me?"

Gaby wrinkles her nose. "Well, you aren't exactly pushing him away."

"Because I thought he had nowhere to go, but he does. I think he's avoiding his old life. I know he never got on with his parents, but he's had friends, flatmates, and he's had Marie."

"Well, they can't see him," Gaby points out.

"True. But he can see them. And I think he avoids all that because it reminds him too much of what he's lost." I sigh deeply. "Emily—the catacomb guide—she said that ghosts flock to me because I make them feel alive."

Gaby immediately puts her arm around me. "They flock to you because you're incredibly kind. You take care of them, so they take care of you. You're just the best."

Smiling, I return the hug. "No, you are. And you deserve someone as funny and great as you. Do you think Marie might be interested?"

Gaby sucks in her lower lip. "I don't know. I think so. I mean, we've flirted a bit, but it could just be banter." Her cheeks glow. "She's cute, isn't she?"

"Yeah, but I'm not sure we should tell her about the ghosts—" My whole body freezes as I notice a darkly dressed figure coming towards us.

"What is it?" Gaby asks, tension in her voice.

"It's him," I whisper, unable to tear my eyes away. "Le Chevalier d'Os."

CHAPTER 16

There is no doubt the Chevalier is here for me. Why else would he leave the catacombs and show up at the Sorbonne? We lock eyes and everything in me wants to scream.

I'm completely stunned, but Gaby grabs my arm and spins me around. "Keep walking."

Our steps lengthen as we head back the way we came. We barely make it twenty metres before a woman steps out of a doorway and points a gun at us.

"Gaby, no!" I pull her back, almost tripping over my own feet.

She gives me a confused look. "What are you doing?"

I stare at the woman with the gun. Her lips curl into a smile as a mad gleam enters her eyes. A madwoman, then.

"Whatever it is, it's not real!" Gaby hisses, tugging on my arm.

"But I am." The Chevalier's deep voice is close to my ear. His hand wraps around my upper arm and pulls me with it.

The woman is a ghost. He sent a ghost to cut me off. I'm angry at myself, confused and scared out of my mind.

Meanwhile, Gaby, who is being dragged along, shouts at the Chevalier: "You can't kidnap us in the middle of the day. We'll scream."

"You're welcome to go," says the Chevalier, sounding amused and not at all concerned about the people on the other side of the road. "But I have business with Alix here."

My bones feel like jelly. I'm probably as pale as a cartoon ghost. "Are you going to kill me?" I whisper.

"Don't be ridiculous. He pushes me and Gaby down onto the edge of a fountain.

Now that winter is approaching, the basin is dry and filled with wet leaves from the surrounding trees. Still, we're in a public place, with hordes of students milling about on their way to and from classes. Surely, he doesn't think he's invincible enough to kill us in front of everyone.

"What do you want?" I ask grumpily now that the immediate danger has receded somewhat.

Gaby clasps my arm as she glares at the man. "I'm not going anywhere."

The Chevalier towers over us. He sneers at Gaby. "Suit yourself." Then his attention falls on me and I feel like I could wither and die on the spot. "I should have known that ghost was yours."

"Who do you mean?" The woman with the gun certainly wasn't one of my acquaintances.

"The boy." The Chevalier gives me a toothy grin. "Your boyfriend, wasn't he?"

A shiver runs down my spine. Before I knew Gaspar was a ghost, I'd mentioned him to the Chevalier. Still... "You said you couldn't see ghosts."

"I can't. But I have my ways." Obviously, he won't tell me any more about it. I suppose it's because he employs ghost whisperers. "So, tell me, Alix. Who are you working for?"

"No one," Gaby blurts out. "She's a student. Unless you mean her part-time job at the Panthéon."

The Chevalier frowns slightly. "Did the ghosts of the Panthéon put you up to this?"

"No," I reply sullenly. "They're not interested in your little schemes."

"My little schemes," he repeats, amused. He puts one foot on the edge beside me and leans on his leg to bring his face closer to mine. "What do you know about my little schemes?"

My mind makes a quick summary. I know he's the head of Nexus—the human side—that he's meeting with cataphiles to explore the catacombs and find places of power, and that he wants the ghost side of Nexus to leave the Boutique of Psychosis. "They killed Emily."

"Who?" He sounds genuinely confused.

A lead weight settles in my stomach and my mouth goes dry. "You don't even know who she was."

"Maybe you could be a bit more specific."

Gaby gasps. "How many people have you murdered that you need a prompt?"

The Chevalier grins at her. "Jumping to conclusions, I see." Then he turns to me. "If you're going to accuse me of murder, you need to tell me who it is I'm supposed to have murdered."

"Emily Durant. She was a tour guide for the catacombs and found your little ritual place in Ossa Arida. I've got pictures." I don't know why I'm threatening a guy who's obviously not above murder, but I don't appreciate the gaslighting. I saw what I saw. "And as soon as I got back from there, *you* were waiting for me with a gun drawn."

Although I just accused him, the Chevalier merely ponders it. "If I remember correctly, I didn't have a gun."

At least he no longer denies that he was there. "Well, your henchwoman then."

"She's a ghost. Her gun can't hurt you. Not really."

"But you just said you can't see ghosts."

He laughs softly. "And I said I have my ways." Still no explanation.

I feel so cold I wrap my arms around my middle. "What about Emily then? She was killed by a real weapon."

"There's nothing to see in Ossa Arida."

"I know."

For the first time, the Chevalier's eyes widen in surprise. "You went back?" He whistles through his teeth. "I seem to have underestimated you, Mademoiselle Alix. I thought I'd scared you off for good, but you came back. And then you sent your ghost friend to spy on me. Impressive."

Gaby jumps to my defence. "She's not some stupid chick, you know?"

"Obviously not." The Chevalier leans closer, and I can't help but lean into Gaby to escape his proximity. "I'll ask you again. Who do you work for?"

This time it's me who says it, though much less forcefully than Gaby did before. "No one." With a sigh I give in. "I do favours for ghosts. Emily asked me to find something of hers in Ossa Arida. She didn't tell me it would be her body until we got there. And Gaspar just wants to protect me. He was right to assume you're a dangerous man."

The Chevalier gives me a pitiful grin. "Aren't we all dangerous?"

"Excuse me?" Gaby exclaims. "We're not the ones running secret communities out of the catacombs, murdering anyone who gets too close, and assaulting young women in the streets."

"The last time I remember, we were talking. And I haven't murdered anyone."

And then, for some reason, the Chevalier lets go of his threatening attitude and just sits down next to me. Gaby immediately moves to the other side so that I don't have to sit so close to him.

If the Chevalier is offended by this, he doesn't show it. Instead, he gives me a rueful smile. "Let's start again, shall we?" He holds out his hand to me. "I'm Romain. Let's keep it on a first-name basis."

I stare at his hand as if it's a venomous snake. "What?" My brain is completely fried. I've registered that the Chevalier has just given me his first name, but everything else is a haze.

He continues to smile. "We got off on the wrong foot. I assume that someone had sent you after me, while you assume that I'm up to no good." His choice of words seems to amuse him. "Nothing could be further from the truth. As it turns out, you and I are in exactly the same business."

"Which is what exactly?" Gaby asks, keeping her thoughts together much better than I am.

"Helping ghosts," the Chevalier—no, Romain—answers in a cheerful voice. He drops his hand when he realises he won't get a handshake. "Look, Alix. I'm a cataphile through and through. I love these old tunnels, the mystery and all that. I also know it's home to so many ghosts." He chuckles softly. "It was quite a surprise to find out how many there were. Or that there were any." His gaze intensifies. "I dream of a shared community away from the social norms of the world above."

Gaby coughs. "The social norm of not murdering innocent people."

Thank god for Gaby's voice of reason. It's far too easy to fall under the Chevalier's spell—I just can't call him Romain in my head. No matter how sweet his words, I can't forget what he's done. Or what he plans to do.

"You say you want to help ghosts and build a community with them. If that's the case, why are you trying to drive the ghosts out of the Boutique of Psychosis?" Would you look at that? I found my brain again. "They weren't very fond of you."

Once again, I managed to surprise him. "Did you really go there? And your mind is still intact?"

I swallow the retort that tries to slip out that my mind is as weird as it ever was. I don't want to bond with this guy. "They're not going to leave."

"Yes, I thought as much."

"So, what's the deal? You work with other ghosts, but not with them?"

The Chevalier grimaces. "It's more a case of *them* not working with me. You see, there are millions of ghosts who call the catacombs home. The Boutique ghosts are just a handful. They despise the idea of working with a mortal."

"They work with me." I probably shouldn't have said that.

"Do they now?" The Chevalier smiles at me. "You continue to surprise me, which makes me want to recruit you even more, I'm afraid. What do I have to do to acquire your talents?"

Leave it to Gaby to jump right in. "Um, she's not for hire. And certainly not for a creep like you."

"What she said?" I reply cautiously.

"Nonsense." The Chevalier shakes his head. "Anyone can be bought. I just have to find out your price." His predatory smile flashes again. "I love a good challenge."

His answer makes me want to puke. All I want is for this guy to leave me alone, but the chances of that seem very slim. But I'd much rather be bought off than coerced by threats. Not that it would make much difference given the power imbalance between us.

Out of the corner of my eye I notice someone else walking straight towards us. "Sébastien!"

I jump up, as if his presence alone gave me the strength to do so. "What are you doing here?"

Next to me, the Chevalier also rises. "I thought you didn't work for anyone." There's a hint of accusation in his voice.

"Isn't he the GoPol agent?" Gaby whispers in my ear. When I nod, she says loudly. "You're police. Arrest this man. He murdered a woman."

I can see that Sébastien is a little overwhelmed by the reaction to his arrival. He stops at a healthy distance from us and glances from

Gaby to the Chevalier before fixing his gaze on me. "What's going on?"

The Chevalier smoothes his dark jacket. "Nothing that concerns you, officer. Or should I say agent?"

"He's le Chevalier d'Os. The one who shot at me," I blurt out.

"I told you it was a ghost. And her weapon is harmless." The Chevalier smiles. "I'm afraid your services aren't required here."

"You murdered Emily Durant?" Sébastien says, his eyes narrowing as he slowly takes control of the situation.

Gaby nods quickly. "Yes, and he threatened Alix."

"There's not a shred of evidence that I was in any way involved in the unfortunate death of a woman I didn't even know," the Chevalier says, as calmly as if we were discussing the weather. I notice that he doesn't exactly deny that he killed Emily.

"She told me you shot her."

I notice that Sébastien's attitude changes slightly. He doesn't have a gun with him, as he's not on a job, but he's obviously had some combat training. Hopefully it won't come to that.

"A ghost told you that," the Chevalier says sweetly, but his smile is directed at Sébastien. "Surely you know that a ghost's confession won't hold up in court, so why don't we save ourselves the embarrassment and leave it at that?"

"But she wasn't always a ghost," Gaby protests. "You have to take him in for questioning." She practically begs Sébastien to do so.

Sébastien's eyes narrow. "There is some proof."

"There is proof of her death," says the Chevalier, amused. "Nothing of my involvement." Then he turns to me. "Alix, if you don't want to work with me, do yourself a favour and stay as far away from GoPol as possible. Believe me, they don't want the best for you."

"You should run from anyone who tells you not to trust the police," Sébastien shoots back.

How did I end up in the middle of a tug-of-war between a special agent and a criminal?

Sébastien comes closer, placing his feet as carefully as a cat on the prowl. No one moves until he's between me and the Chevalier. Behind me, Gaby breathes a sigh of relief. "Stay away from her."

The Chevalier's smile doesn't falter. "I'm not the dangerous one here, Agent Roubert. It's your father and his plans you should be worried about." His grin deepens. "But then again, who knows that better than you?" He nods at me over Sébastien's shoulder. "See you around, Alix. Think about what you want."

And with that, the Chevalier walks away as if he didn't have a care in the world.

CHAPTER 17

Gaby is furious with Sébastien for letting le Chevalier d'Os go. "You should have arrested him!"

"I couldn't have done that," explains Sébastien. "I'm not a policeman. And even if I were, he was right, there is no reason to arrest him. Nothing that would have stood up in court."

"There must be something you can do!" Gaby looks at me. "Alix has testified about his involvement. Surely that's worth something. And if you do some digging, you'll find some real evidence."

"Alix didn't really testify to anything." He checks with me. "You didn't go to the police, did you?"

"I thought I had." When Sébastien found me after my encounter with the Chevalier in Ossa Arida, I told him everything I knew. Until now, I'd assumed that meant I'd already done my civic duty. The Chevalier's words come back to me. He told me to run away from GoPol.

Sébastien sighs. "We handle these things quietly within GoPol."

"Why?" Gaby demands to know.

"Because of the ghosts," says Sébastien, beginning to sound a little exasperated. "As soon as ghosts are involved in any way, it becomes a GoPol case. There's no need to send ordinary officers to chase ghost testimonies. If we'd found Emily's body the way Alix left it, we might have had a case, but not like this."

Gaby crosses her arms and glares at him. "This is bullshit."

"Maybe, but I don't make the rules."

"That's right." She squints her eyes. "Your father does. What was that all about?"

Sébastien gives me such a helpless look I feel compelled to intervene. "Gaby, it's alright." I put a hand on her shoulder and reassure her. "I know this has all been very frightening, but the danger has passed. The Chevalier was just trying to get into our heads to get us to trust him, that's all."

Gaby grumbles, but she seems to accept my intervention. "That sounds like him. Is there anything you can do to stop him visiting Alix? I don't feel safe if he knows where to find her."

"Has he threatened you?" Sébastien looks worried.

"He brought a ghost with a gun. I didn't know what it was until he told me, and I was already in control of the situation. Other than that, no, not explicitly." I'm incredibly embarrassed that this has happened to me again. When will I finally learn to recognise ghosts straight away?

"If we knew his name—" Sébastien muses.

"Romain," Gaby blurts out.

Sébastien waits for her to say more, but she doesn't. That's all we know. He sighs. "It's not enough for a restraining order. If you want, you can go to the police with this and a description, but they probably won't be able to do much."

Horrified, Gaby stumbles back. "So, you're not going to do anything?"

"I didn't say that," Sébastien protests. "But short of following Alix wherever she goes, I don't know what to do at the moment."

"Still bullshit," Gaby grumbles, and I tend to agree.

The idea of having Sébastien follow me everywhere I go isn't particularly appealing. "He seems more interested in working with me."

Sébastien immediately warns me, "Don't!"

"I wasn't going to." Man, people have to show me some respect. I may be too curious for my own good, but I'm not stupid.

"Does this have something to do with Jacques de Molay?" Sébastien suddenly asks.

"No, nothing at all."

Gaby squeezes my arm. "Can I trust you with him?" She looks at Sébastien. "I really need to go to the bathroom after that scare."

"Of course." Despite what the Chevalier said, Sébastien seems perfectly fine.

"I'll see you in class later." The look she gives Sébastien promises thunder and rain if he betrays her trust.

But he only seems to find it amusing. "She's very protective of you, isn't she?"

"Very." I wouldn't know what to do without Gaby in my life.

Sébastien smiles. "Good, but it won't be enough.'"

Way to pump up the drama. "What do you mean? Enough for what?"

"To protect you if you continue to get involved with all these ghosts and people who deal with ghosts."

I sit down by the fountain again and Sébastien joins me. "I've been working with ghosts for about fifteen years. I have never needed protection."

"What do you work with them for?" He seems genuinely confused. "What about Jacques de Molay? He asked you to do this, didn't he? To prove his legitimacy?"

"Did Cédric tell you that?"

Sébastien rolls his eyes at me. "Yes, he did. Thought I wanted to know."

"Well, obviously he was right about that."

"I'm just worried about you," Sébastien confesses. "You keep putting yourself at risk without any protection."

"Are you really offering to stay here?"

He winces. "I can't. I have a job to do." Then he sighs heavily. "It's important you find your own ghost. You see, they're different from the others. With one foot in the living world, our ghosts can actually protect us. It's not a bulletproof vest, but since they can influence the mortal world to some extent, it's something. That's why I'm so anxious for you to find it."

As interesting as that is, I don't really see the point. "I thought my ghost was an infant at best."

"It's still important that you reconnect with her." He seems so serious, I should probably spend some more energy on it. If it can help me stay safe in the catacombs, it's certainly a good thing. "So, why are you helping this Molay guy? Hasn't he been dead for six centuries?"

"Seven. And I'm helping him because he asked me to." It's really not that difficult. On the other hand, Victor mentioned that I'm unique for doing this. "Just because he's been dead for seven centuries doesn't mean he's stopped feeling. You know what ghosts are like. They're just like us, only dead."

Sébastien winces at the comparison. "I wouldn't say that."

"Why not?"

"Well, because they're nothing like us. They don't have jobs—or needs for that matter. They don't feel the passage of time like we do, and they tend to work in patterns. The older they are, the more fragmented these patterns become. They're ghosts, Alix, not real people."

I wonder if that's something they tell people in GoPol. "That's not my experience. They feel the passage of time more than we do,

I'd say. If you spent some time with the ghosts of the Panthéon, you'd see what I mean. It's true they can't leave their mark on the world like they used to, but that doesn't stop them from wanting things. And Molay wants to be recognised for who he was. The last Grand Master of the Templars, unjustly burned at the stake. He belongs in the Panthéon."

Sébastien looks at me sceptically. "And moving his remains from one crypt to another would make him happier?"

"Why wouldn't it?" I smile wistfully. "Right now, he's resentful. Seven centuries of being accused of terrible misdeeds, with no grave or monument to properly commemorate him. Giving him his due, however late, will make the rest of his existence much more pleasant."

He considers my words. Finally, he shakes his head. "I still don't think it's worth the risk, but it's not my decision to make."

"It isn't," I say, a little too pointedly. "And I'd appreciate it if you didn't use your cousin to spy on me."

"I haven't," he says, as mortified as I am. "I swear. Cédric thinks he'll get into GoPol if he teams up with me. He won't. My father doesn't think he's qualified. And he's not. He's as blind to ghosts as anybody else." With a sigh, Sébastien stands up. "I can't stop you helping Molay. I still think it's useless, but if it makes you happy, I suppose there's no harm in it. Just be careful down there. And find your ghost."

I'm tempted to salute him. Instead, I just promise to be care-ful—and to put finding my ghost self at the top of my list.

Chapter 18

It seems I'll never get to my class, because as soon as I enter the Sorbonne, I notice someone else following me. At first, I assume it's Sébastien, but then I notice the change in clothing and manner and realise it's his ghost, Dix. Is this Sébastien's way of making sure I'm protected, or does Dix have his own agenda?

I use my knowledge of the university and duck into a corner where there are only a few old cupboards under a staircase. When Dix follows me, I confront him directly. "What are you doing here?"

He gives me a rueful smile. "When did you notice?"

"From the moment I walked in. Have you been there the whole time?"

"Yeah, pretty much." He scratches the back of his neck and wrinkles his nose in typical teenage fashion.

It's possible I didn't notice him at the fountain because I was so preoccupied with everything else that was happening, but it reminds me of how he appeared in Ossa Arida when I needed help and not a minute before. "How come I don't see you all the time?"

"Special perks of being a whisper ghost," he says with a grin. "We can hide from ghosts and whisperers alike if we want to. Very helpful. But you noticed me."

I cross my arms and give him a long look. "Did I? Or did you want me to notice you?"

Dix shows me his pearly whites with a broad grin. "I like you."

I don't know what to make of him. The fact that he's Sébastien and yet not the least bit like him is confusing, but maybe I can use this to get some questions answered. "Why are you following me?"

Dix gives me a one-sided shrug. "I heard what you said about ghosts and found it interesting."

"How so?" Is he going to tell me I'm wrong too?

"That we have feelings too." The grin finally falters. "That's not what GoPol encourages."

I suddenly feel sorry for him. Sébastien sees him as a tool when they should have been partners, and I'm reminded that Dix died at seventeen. "What's their deal anyway?"

The smile he gives me is only a ghost of the previous one. "I can't tell you. It's classified information, you know? I don't know why Séb is so open with you, but we've been trained better than that."

"You have? Since when did you train for GoPol?" There is a small inconsistency that has been bothering me all along about this family of ghost whisperers.

The real grin returns, and I have the feeling I asked the right question. "Oh, forever, really. It was a great game at first, but where other parents sent their kids to football training, we were sent to martial arts. Which was cool and not terribly unique, but that was just the physical training. There's also the rules." He rolls his eyes. "All those rules! So annoying. But Séb loves them. He's such a good little soldier, isn't he? Papa's little darling."

Okay, I'm confused. "Aren't you Séb...astien?"

"No, not anymore. We've been separated for eight years. I hardly recognise him these days, and I spend almost every waking minute of his with him."

I've got so many questions, and it looks like Dix is more than happy to answer them. More than Sébastien is, despite his apparent openness towards me. "So, the plan was always to join GoPol? How lucky that you died then, right?" I try to sound casual, but my insides are churning at the monstrosity of it all.

"Yes, very lucky." The sarcasm drips from Dix's reply. There is no need to spell it out now.

I swallow hard before I dare to whisper, "How did you die?"

"Look, Alix." Dix glances over his shoulder and lowers his voice as if anyone but me could hear him. "The less you know, the better. I don't know what Séb's plan is for you."

"There's a plan?" Damn it! I wanted to trust Sébastien.

"There's always a plan at GoPol. We don't do things on a whim. Not like you." Dix looks me up and down with a sense of admiration. "Why do you really help ghosts? What's in it for you?"

I get it now. When GoPol interacts with ghosts, it's for their own purposes. They use them as spies, as messengers. They treat them as tools, even their own whisper spirits, not as the people they once were. "I help ghosts because no one else will," I say quietly. "Until recently, I thought it was because no one else could. That I was the only one who could see and hear them. The only one they could turn to. If I can help, why shouldn't I? Why should I ignore their suffering? Even if it's the smallest thing. If I can help them, why not?"

"But this thing with Molay isn't small," Dix points out. "He's a frightening man."

"No, it's quite big. But it's also important. There is so much pain, so much injustice in what happened to him. If I can right a few wrongs, then it's worth it, isn't it?"

Dix looks at me with a kind of hunger in his eyes. It's as if he's hanging on my every word.

I decide to take a chance. "Do you need a favour, Dix?" Sure, I said Molay would be my last, but if Dix needs me to talk to Sébastien, I won't say no.

He swallows hard. Even though his body shouldn't be able to produce spit, the old manner is still there. "No." He pulls away.

"No, I'm fine. Just... just be careful, okay. We don't want to lose you."

And before I can ask him if the "we" he's referring to is him and Sébastien, or a wider group like all ghosts, he disappears before my eyes, not even giving me the courtesy of walking away.

With a sigh, I put my rucksack down and leave the corner, only to run straight into Théo. As always, he looks at me with a mixture of disgust and confusion. "You're so weird, you know."

Normally I'd have Gaby standing up for me and telling him and his friends off, but I don't really need her. With everything that's happened today and in general, Théo is really the least of my problems. "So what?"

"What do you mean, 'so what'?"

"I'm weird. Who cares?" I narrow my eyes. "Why do *you* care?"

Théo scoffs dejectedly. "I don't." He strides off, as if he can't get away from me fast enough, even though we're going to the exact same lecture.

I don't care anymore. Let him think I'm weird. He's just a boy who has no idea what's really going on in the world. My ghosts are real, and now there's proof. If he's got a problem with that, it's not my concern. I'm done hiding what I am.

CHAPTER 19

There's a spell of good weather at the end of the week. I decide to take Malou for a walk with Gaspar and visit my grandmother in Père Lachaise. But this isn't just a social call. Sébastien's warning still lives rent-free in my head, giving me an urgency to find my whisper ghost.

But I'm not doing it because of him. I firmly believe that no toddler ghost is going to be able to help me, and even if they could, I wouldn't put them in harm's way like that. Talking to Dix made one thing clear to me. The whisper ghosts, as he called them, were separated from our lives, stuck in a younger stage forever. But like any other ghost, they still feel and hope, and that means that somewhere in Paris there is a little girl, all alone in the world, abandoned by everyone she relied on.

Night is falling early this late in November, which makes Père Lachaise even more beautiful in my eyes. Wrought iron lanterns cast a soft orange glow on the pathways, illuminating the tombstones, small fences, and offerings to the dead. As usual, it's a busy place. I suppose some of the evening strollers are alive, but most are dead. There are a few children among them, but none that look like a glimpse of the past.

Malou dodges the ghosts as well as I do, while taking a keen interest in the weeds growing at the side of the path. She's probably looking for some of the bugs that play their buzzing night songs. It's a lovely night for a walk, almost like a date. But this isn't a date. Gaspar and I are just friends. After I told him what happened with the Chevalier, Sébastien, and Dix, he insisted on staying for my protection, in place of the whisper ghost I don't have.

"What if they're wrong and there is no whisper ghost?" Gaspar asks. "From what I've seen so far, GoPol don't seem to have a very good understanding of what ghosts are or what they want. They could be wrong."

I considered that, but who says I'm an expert? "They've been around a lot longer than me, I suppose. They've probably been studying this for decades, if not centuries."

"But it doesn't add up," protests Gaspar. "If what they say is true, there should be thousands, maybe millions of ghost whisperers. The existence of ghosts wouldn't be a secret. I mean, I know there are a lot of people who believe in ghosts, like Marie, but not in this kind of afterlife. Not like you. But people are brought back from the dead every day with modern medicine, so shouldn't there be a whole bunch of ghost whisperers around?"

He's right. It doesn't add up. And yet it's definitely true for Sébastien and Dix. Though not confirmed, their death seemed to have been a planned step in the training process. I still shudder to think about it. Was Sébastien really so desperate to please his father that he'd flirt with death? I suppose desperation runs in the family, and teenage brains aren't exactly known for making good, healthy choices.

"Look, I'll just ask my grandmother, and if she doesn't know anything either, we'll go with your theory. My mother doesn't seem to remember what happened—*if* anything happened—or is unwilling to tell me. Whether that's out of shame or because she's banished it from her mind, I don't know. But if she has chosen to keep it secret, my father will most likely do the same. So, I'm turning to the one adult I can be sure won't keep secrets from me."

We've almost reached my grandmother's section when someone calls my name. I look up and see a familiar figure walking towards us. Peter Abelard.

He gives us a brief nod, his eyes full of sadness. "I was hoping to see you again."

"Is there anything I could do for you?" I ask, assuming he's come to ask for my help, like so many ghosts before him.

"Oh no." He shakes his head. "There is nothing that can help me these days." Even his smile is sad. "I've come to apologise."

Intrigued, I wrap Malou's leash around my hand so she won't suddenly slip out of my grasp. "Apologise for what?"

"The last time we met, I didn't show you my best side."

"That's okay. Ghosts are allowed to have bad days too." I look at Gaspar, who's had plenty of bad days as a ghost, coming to terms with his new existence.

Abelard snorts quietly. "That may be, but that doesn't give us the right to treat others unkindly or to strike fear into their hearts. Especially not when they're still alive, able to take their fate into their own hands and change it." His smile disappears completely, and he frowns, looking down at us like an old teacher who doesn't like his pupil's handwriting. "The truth is, Mademoiselle Alix, that it is not pleasant to love another from afar, nor is it wise to cling to hope when all hope is in vain."

My throat tightens as I take in his words. I know there's no hope for me and Gaspar. That's why I've given up on him romantically.

"But the heart won't listen to reason," Abelard continues. "It is an unreliable and incorrigible traitor to reason." The smile returns. "Neither distance nor reason is ever enough of an obstacle to what the heart wants. So don't listen to me. Open yourself, embrace the pain and enjoy it, because that's what it's all about in the end. That's all that matters, whether you're dead or alive."

"How can you enjoy something that has no future?" I gasp, not realising I've just said the words out loud. I don't want the pain that comes with loving Gaspar. "There is no point."

Abelard grimaces. "Point or no point, the feelings won't go away. I still long for a child. Some days the lack of it is unbearable. I still have so much love to give. Other times I'm at peace with it. But the longing never goes away, it's a part of me—and of Héloïse." His eyes burn with fervour as he turns the conversation back to me and Gaspar. "You still have options, Alix. You can run from the pain and try to replace it, or you can embrace it and make it your own. Just don't ever lose hope, because that's what keeps us here, tied to this world for as long as it will have us." He glances at Gaspar, as if only now realising that his advice was directed at me alone. "You'll learn to exist with it, boy."

Gaspar's cheek twitches. "I hear that a lot." He straightens his shoulders. "But you're right, it's not my choice to make. Alix is young and I'm dead. It is what it is. I never had the chance to have anything with her. All I can give her is my friendship and support. And that's fine. I'm okay with that, really. Because I know she deserves so much more than what I can be to her."

Tears run down my cheeks. I wipe them away angrily. I was over it. I really thought I was over the whole thing with Gaspar, that we'd somehow come to a new understanding with a healthy distance. But if anything, our relationship has only deepened. We have removed the physical aspects of it, but the emotional ones are rooted deeper every time we get together. And it doesn't matter that we've never met in real life. This is real. And unless I make a proper decision, we will be stuck in this limbo for the rest of my life.

Abelard seems to know what I'm thinking. He and Héloïse are prime examples of never letting go of each other. They've lived longer apart than together. And although they spend eternity in each other's arms, the happiness of a fulfilled life eludes them. And that's the real tragedy of their love story.

He gives me a knowing look before taking his leave. "Whatever you choose to do in life, make every moment count."

As Abelard makes his way back up the hill, Gaspar tries to take my hand. I pull away and immediately regret it when I see his face fall. "Sorry," I whisper.

Gaspar buries his hands in his hoodie. "Let's go see your grandma, shall we?"

I love him even more for giving me the space I need. For the millionth time I regret that we didn't meet before he died. At least then I could have claimed the benefit of grief, instead of having to pretend that there was never anything of substance.

Together we walk through the cemetery until we reach my grandmother's grave. Like the other day, she and Beatrice are delighted to see Gaspar. My grandmother pats the gravestone next to her and calls Gaspar over. "Come, young man. We didn't get a chance to talk much last time. I'm Estelle, Alix's grandmother."

I lean against Beatrice's gravestone as I watch my grandmother pepper Gaspar with questions, like why he's painting his nails or whether he ever wears a nice shirt instead of those hideous hoodies. For a moment it seems as if they find common ground in their love of music, but the kind of music Gaspar listens to is nothing but noise to my grandmother.

"If she goes on like this, she won't like him anymore," I say to Beatrice.

The old woman laughs. "Oh, dearie. Old crones like us love to judge the young. It's a pastime. In the end, only two things matter to her. That he's a good man and treats you well, and that you care about him." She smiles triumphantly. "Besides, I rather like his anti-establishment flair. Very revolutionary."

Gaspar somehow survives the intense questioning and begins to ask some questions of his own about the ghost community at Père Lachaise, which my grandmother answers in far more detail than necessary, and after a while they actually seem to get along quite well.

When Malou, who has been busy clearing the area of bugs, comes over and tugs on my shoelace as if to ask when we're going home, I clear my throat. "Sorry to interrupt, but I was wondering if you could tell me something."

My grandmother immediately turns her attention to me. "What is it, darling?"

"Maman won't tell me anything, but I'm almost one hundred percent sure that I had a bad accident in my early childhood. Do you know anything about it?" I won't explain the whole ghost whisperer theory that GoPol has put together, because we don't really know if it's true.

"A bad accident?"

"Yes. Bad enough that I had to be resuscitated or spend time in hospital."

My grandmother frowns. "Why would you think that?" But before I can come up with any kind of explanation, something occurs to her. "Oh no... Look, I don't know anything about an accident per se, but I *do* remember that there was a time when your sister—Hélène, of course—was very upset. She must have been seven or so, but she wouldn't tell me anything, just that we had to keep you safe. She was very worried about you for a few weeks. Maybe you should ask Léni?"

I had hoped it wouldn't come to this, but it seems I have no choice. A visit to my sister seems in order.

CHAPTER 20

You know your sister has made it when she can afford to rent a normal-sized apartment in downtown Paris. Compared to Gaby's little shoebox flat, this one is almost as big as my family's, with a proper bathroom and kitchen, a living room, a bedroom, and a spare room that is now used as an office but could easily be converted into a nursery in a few years' time.

I don't fail to notice that it's near the restaurant Sébastien invited me to. And if I remember correctly, she also works not far from here. Her job obviously pays well enough, or at least, together with Cédric, she can afford this place. It's a far cry from anything I'll ever be able to afford if I stay in Paris, and there's no way I'm leaving this bustling necropolis behind.

I gave Hélène half an hour's notice before turning up on her doorstep. Either she keeps her place spotless or she's the fastest panic cleaner in history. The display of sheer perfection makes my nose itch. Lately, I seem to find it harder and harder to accept my older sibling's superiority.

"Alix!" my sister exclaims, as if surprised to see me after the warning I'd given her. "What brings you here?"

Before I can answer, Cédric comes out of the kitchen with a cheesy smile on his face. "It's so nice to have you for dinner. I hope you like gnocchi."

"Gnocchi?" I don't see anything wrong with it, but apparently it needs special attention.

Hélène smiles warmly. "Cédí is in his Italian phase."

Oh dear, I'm beginning to regret my decision to visit Happy Couplelandia. They're hard to take on a good day, even harder when my own love life is a gigantic mess. "Awesome. Looking forward to it. Can I talk to you?" I ask my sister with a sense of urgency. I had hoped that tonight would be one of the nights that Cédric would be at work, but as usual the two of them are a package deal.

"Sure. Let's set the table and open a bottle of wine."

I get involved in preparing the dining table, which is placed in front of the best view in the apartment. From here you can see the Eiffel Tower rising between the buildings. Fairy lights have been strung across the window frame and there's an old-fashioned candleholder on the table.

"Am I interrupting your date?" I ask, feeling a little guilty.

Hélène laughs. "Every night is a date night," she says, making me cringe. She immediately rolls her eyes. "Cédric's words, not mine."

Her annoyed tone gives me the slightest hint that my real sister is still in there somewhere, so I give her a teasing grin. "Don't pretend you're not lapping it all up."

She wrinkles her nose and squints at me. "And what's wrong with that?"

"Nothing," I say, still amused. "Just that you got what you always wanted."

Hélène pours three glasses of red wine. "And what is it that you want?"

I decide I'd rather not go into that now and get to the point of my visit, as it's not exactly dinner conversation. "Sébastien told me that ghost whisperers like us are made—so to speak—after a near-death experience."

This apparently requires her to sit down. "What?"

"The reason I can see ghosts—according to him—is because I had a brush with death at some point in my early childhood. I basically died and became a ghost, but then I was brought back to life. Cue magical ghost-seeing powers." If I sound flippant, it's because I don't want to get into the emotional crap with her.

Hélène closes her eyes, clearly trying to remain calm. When she opens her eyes again, she calls out, "Cédric?"

"Really? Can't you just take my word for it? You need *him* to confirm it?"

"*He's* going to be my husband," Hélène hisses.

"I wouldn't have taken you for the submissive type." If we're at that point, Hélène is well and truly lost.

She pulls her face in indignation. "How dare you? We have a partnership. There's nothing wrong with sharing information in a relationship."

"There is when you share my information." I almost say that we used to be in a partnership too, but then Cédric comes in.

"Sorry, I had to take care of the sauce first," he announces. "What's up, ladies?"

I almost throw up in my mouth. Hélène gives me an ominous look, which I return with a sullen one. She sighs and almost throws her hands up in the air. "Um, Alix told me about this ghost thing, and I just want to make sure I understand it correctly. You're the expert, so what was it, Alix?" Her question is pointed enough to stab me in the back.

"All my life I've been telling you about ghosts and now Cédric is the expert?"

Hélène looks embarrassed for a mere second. "Well, his family has worked for GoPol for several generations," she argues. "I'm not saying your experience isn't valid, but you've just gone with the flow. Cédric and Sébastien have learnt all this the right way. Right?"

She looks for help from her husband-to-be, who seems rather amused by the whole situation. He leans over to pick up the third glass of wine and takes a sip before asking me. "What exactly did you want to know?"

"Nothing." I cluck my tongue, annoyed because there is something I want to know. I try to calm myself with a sigh. "I told Hélène what Sébastien told me." If she doesn't believe me, hopefully a reminder of where this information comes from will snap her out of this insulting attitude. "You have to die to become a ghost whisperer. I don't know if your heart has to stop, or if you have to stop breathing, but in those few seconds or minutes when you are technically dead, a ghost is formed, and when you're brought back from the dead by CPR, or a shot of adrenaline, or defib, or whatever, you wake up as a ghost whisperer."

Cédric stares at me, taking far too long to absorb all the information.

My sister doesn't have the patience for this. "Is that true?"

Nope, he did not know that.

"Um..." Cédric takes another deep sip. "If Sébastien says so, I suppose so. Yes."

Smugly, I turn to my sister, projecting, *"Who's the expert now?"*

Of course, she'd never go back on her word. "Okay, that's a bit scary." She, too, drowns out the awkwardness with some red wine.

"Speaking of creepy, Grandma said you might know when that happened to me, because I can't remember a near-death experience and Maman won't tell me anything."

"Grandma said?" Hélène looks as if she is going to faint. "What has Grandma Louise got to do with it?"

"Not Grandma Louise. Papa's mother, Estelle."

She breathes flatly in and out. "You still talk to her?"

It's been so long since Hélène was on board with the whole ghost thing, I'd almost forgotten she used to ask me about Grandma Estelle all the time. I cross my arms. "Just because you stopped visiting her doesn't mean I had to abandon her."

"Alix, please."

I hold back my anger for now, but it's only fair after she's undermined my experience once again for some man's opinion. "Anyway, was there an accident that might fit the bill? Grandma mentioned you were obsessed with keeping me safe for a while."

Hélène snorts. "When am I not? Not that it makes any difference."

"Interesting interpretation, but sure. Is there a moment you can remember that made you even more obsessed?"

Instead of getting lost in our sisterly bickering again, Hélène leans back and sits with her wine glass, thinking.

Meanwhile, Cédric half turns towards the corridor. "Look, I could check the records for any reported incidents if you want. Let me just get on with the gnocchi first."

Why is it that my future brother-in-law is proving so much more helpful than my apparently oh-so-worried sister? Cédric is really stepping up his game lately. I'm just not sure why he's suddenly so interested.

It's only when we hear him rattling with the pots in the kitchen that Hélène snaps out of her thoughts. She glances out into the hallway before getting up and closing the door. I'm not sure this will keep Cédric out, but I'm willing to listen.

"I think you were about three years old," she says in a low voice. "Maman took us girls for a walk along the Seine. She used to love looking in the shops for a bargain or an odd piece of art. Then she bumped into a friend of hers and they started talking while you and I played tag on the promenade. It was your turn, but there were so many people. I think you tried to dodge them when…" Hélène takes a deep breath, clearly struggling with the memories.

My own mind is blank. I've walked along the Seine countless times in my life with different people. But I cannot remember this particular day. Or ever visiting the place with my maman when I was younger.

"You fell," Hélène admits in a whisper, tears in her eyes. "I heard you scream, but I didn't see you. I looked for you, but someone pushed me back from the edge." She shudders, then recovers. "There were so many people. Someone jumped in after you. It must have been really quick, but it felt like forever before they pulled you out. I remember how small you were on the ground, surrounded by so many people. And then Maman, who was crying and panicking because you obviously weren't breathing. But then they gave you CPR, and you threw up all this water and you were fine."

Hélène blinks several times and looks up, trying to keep the tears away. "You recovered so quickly. I think you were more shocked by all the people around us than by what had happened, but I never forgot how still your body was on the stone."

I get up from my chair and put my arms around Hélène. She's startled, shocked at the sudden affection, but then she returns the hug. "So that's when it started?"

It seems that Sébastien was right after all. I *did* have a near-death experience when I was younger. One that I don't remember, while my mother refuses to remember it.

"I didn't realise I was seeing ghosts until I met Beatrice. Remember her, Grandma's best friend in the cemetery?" I feel Hélène nod against my chest. "She's the first one I knew was dead, but I probably saw her before."

"They look like normal people to you, don't they?" Hélène whispers.

I lean back a little and nod. "Yes. It leads to a lot of embarrassing situations when I don't notice." Like falling in love with a guy who died in a horrible accident.

Hélène lets go of me. She wipes her cheeks and empties her glass. "Well, you seem to be enjoying some part of it."

At the moment I can't really see the joy in it, but then I think of all the wonderful friendships I've made with people from all across different eras. "Yes. Yes, I do."

She takes a deep breath, probably pushing away all her protests and arguments to focus on the important part. "I never want to see you like this again," she whispers, just as Cédric knocks on the door, his hands probably full of food.

As she gets up to open it for him, I think about her words. Perhaps I have been a little hard on her lately. All her worries come from a place of love. They're suffocating, but for a good reason. I don't want to imagine what it must be like to fear for the life of someone you love at such a young age.

But now I know that Sébastien was right and that I really must find my ghost. Hélène had twenty years to come to terms with her traumatic memories. The little girl left in the Seine hasn't had the privilege of growing up. It's time to pull her out of the water.

Chapter 21

The dry weather continues. I persuade Gaby to join me for a walk along the Seine. Hélène couldn't remember exactly where it happened, so I resigned myself to a long day. Now that it's winter, there are only a few street artists and stalls braving the weather, and even fewer customers. The accident must have happened in the summer months when the sidewalks are crowded with tourists. It's not much to go on, but knowing how far along the Seine the stalls are usually spread helps to narrow down our search area somewhat.

As promised, Gaspar is there for protection, but he keeps to himself, walking two paces behind us while I chat to Gaby. We may be looking for my deceased younger self, but her mind is somewhere else entirely.

"So, I was thinking of casually inviting Marie to go clubbing... with you," she adds with a hopeful smile.

"You want me to go clubbing?" It wouldn't be the first time, but apart from the rave with Gaspar, I've never really enjoyed this kind of outing.

Gaby laughs slightly embarrassed, her cheeks turning red. "Well, I thought that would make it easier. You know, if you... or both of us invited her to a girls' night out, you know. We could say it's to take your mind and hers off Gaspar, instead of making it a date."

I give her a long look. "But it is a date."

"Well, I don't know. I mean, I don't even know if she'd be interested in something like that. Or if she likes me."

I look over my shoulder at Gaspar, silently seeking his expertise on Marie's love life.

For a moment he pretends he hasn't been listening, but then he sighs. "Look, I don't know. She had a boyfriend some time ago, but they broke up. Apparently, she's quite religious. The Maltesers are religious, aren't they?"

"True."

"What's true?" Gaby asks. "Did you ask Gaspar?"

I pat her arm, comforting her. "I did. He doesn't know, but he reminded me that she grew up in a Malteser household."

"Oh yes. I wonder what that was like. I mean, I have to admit I went down the rabbit hole after our meeting with Paul. The Order of Malta is a sovereign state without a real country. They lost their seat in Malta some time ago and most of their members are ordinary citizens. Like her uncle or Marie, herself, if she is a member at all. They do have some strange structures though, like nobility has only recently been removed as a deciding factor in the upper echelons." Gaby takes a rare breath as a new thought crosses her mind. "Do you think Marie is some kind of princess?"

"The princess of pain au chocolat, maybe," Gaspar sneers, and I can't help but giggle.

Gaby groans, thinking I'm making fun of her. "I know I'm being silly by obsessing over this girl I've only met once or twice. But she's really cute, you know."

"If you say so." I pat her arm again. Marie is quite pretty. I could definitely see her with Gaby, but this is far from the first crush she's ever had, and most of them never come to fruition. "We'll ask her out. I can even take one for the team, if it makes it more casual."

Gaby squeals. "You're the best! This weekend is a bit late, but maybe next weekend?"

"Next weekend sounds good." If her plan succeeds, Gaby and Marie will hit it off and I'm in for a long night alone in a crowded club. But this is Gaby we're talking about. My best friend would never let that happen.

If all goes well, the night will go exactly as planned and take my mind off Gaspar. If it goes badly, the whole atmosphere will remind me of that amazing first date we had at the rave, the one I really went to alone.

I'm about to make a second confirmation when I hear a small child's scream, followed by a splash. Without thinking, I run to the edge. The Seine is grey under a cloudy sky, its current moving the water rapidly downstream. There! A head bobs up, a little mouth gasps for air.

Without a moment's hesitation, I throw down my bag and shrug off my coat and shoes.

"Alix!" Gaby shrieks. "What are you doing?"

"There's a child—" I look back. There's a child in the water, but no adult around. I'm looking at a ghost. Probably my ghost.

"Remember, she's already dead."

The little girl's cry rips my heart out. "Mam—!" The rest of the word is lost in a gurgle. The fear she feels as the river takes her away cuts through the fog of my memories. I died in there.

"She still needs help." I jump into the water, feet first.

It's not safe to swim in the Seine. There's a lot of rubbish in the river, both from boats and from nearby households. I try not to think about it too much as I swallow a mouthful of river water.

I deliberately jumped in a few metres away from the ghost child so I wouldn't land on its head. It takes me a moment to orientate myself. When I spot what looks like a hand raised for help, I start swimming towards it.

Waves crash over my head, taking me completely under. The water is cold, much colder than I had expected. I know I have to be quick if I want to save the child—from drowning and from hypothermia.

I should have reached them by now, but I can't see them anywhere. Panic rises in my throat as I feel the weight of my clothes pulling me down with the current. What if she's already sunk? There's no one to save her. I dive down to see if I can see her, but the Seine is so murky and the water so cold that it only stings my eyes.

I swallow another mouthful of water, and when I come up for air, I don't break the surface, but take another gulp. My arms and legs flail about as I try to work out which way is up and which way is down. Too many forces are pulling me in all sorts of directions, and I can't trust any of them.

The rescue mission is forgotten as my foggy memories come to the fore, bringing with them a terrible fear. I don't know which is me and which is the ghost. All I know is I have to breathe! I want to open my mouth, but I know I shouldn't. Not until I'm back on the surface. If only I knew which way it was.

My lungs are starting to hurt and the temptation to just open my mouth is getting stronger every second. The cold feels like pins and needles, while my clothes seem to be made of chainmail. I'm struggling to remember why I'm in the water at all, when I could have been nice and dry on the shore.

My mind. That's right. I was trying to save my ghost. Where is it? Where is anything?

I suddenly break the surface as someone pulls me through the water. The air rushes back into my lungs and I come up spluttering. Somehow, I find myself much further downstream than where I jumped in.

"Alix!" Gaby's frantic call reaches me from high above. "I'll throw you a ring. Just stay up."

But I don't need to wait, because the force that has pulled me out of the depths is Gaspar. And while Gaby can't see him, he can pull me back to the shore without ever tiring. "I've got you," he promises.

A life ring sails over my head. By then Gaspar has pulled me back to the shore and is helping me climb a rusty ladder at river level.

Even with his help, it's hard work getting my cold, wet body out of the water. When I finally manage, I collapse on the stone with my feet dangling over the edge.

But Gaspar won't let me. "Come on, Alix. You need to get up and move." He grabs my hands and pulls my unwilling body to a standing position.

Just as I'm being pulled back down, Gaby runs at me full speed, wraps her arms around me and slams me to the floor. "Oh my god, Alix! You're alive!"

"Not for long if she doesn't get out of those wet clothes," Gaspar grumbles. But while he was able to pull me out of the water using my ghost whisperer powers, he can't do anything about Gaby, not even make her listen to him.

I should probably help him. Or help myself. "Clothes. Gaby. I need clothes." That's not exactly what I wanted to say, but she seems to understand immediately.

"Oh, yes. Quick, take off your trousers and top. We can dry you off with my scarf, and I'll lend you my jumper. Then I'll get your things and we'll find a café to warm you up."

We do as she says and divide the rest of our clothes evenly between us. I'm still cold and parts of me are still wet, but I'm also warm enough to feel the bite of the cold again. Gaspar stays with us until he sees me happily settled in a café with a hot coffee and the promise of towels.

There's a bit of a commotion. People are checking up on me and wondering what I was thinking. Embarrassed, I explain that it was an accident. Since no one saw me jump in, I get away with a few shakes of the head and stern words.

When things have finally calmed down, Gaby whispers, "What did you see?"

"Myself." I could slap myself for jumping into action without really thinking through the consequences. My ghostly self is already dead, I'm not. "It was me. Or if not me, then some other child who *actually* died in the floods, however long ago." I reject this theory. Our connection was too strong to be anything else.

I look out the window and realise how close we are to Île de la Cité, the place where Jacques de Molay met his end. But where he died in the flames of apparent justice, I had almost drowned in the icy floods. A shiver runs down my spine that has nothing to do with hypothermia. It almost feels as if our fates are somehow connected.

"You found your ghost?" Gaby keeps her voice so low that I would have had trouble understanding her if I hadn't known exactly what she was asking.

I shrug with a sigh. "I don't know. There was a child in the water. I thought... Actually, I didn't think. I just jumped. Like always."

She puts her hand on mine and smiles. "That's what I love about you, Alix. How many people do you think jump in like that?"

"None, because they don't see things," I answer bitterly.

But Gaby shakes her head. "It doesn't matter. We know that what you see is real. What I mean is that not many people are brave enough or selfless enough to help others in need. I mean, how many ghosts have you helped?"

"I didn't help this one."

"I'm sure the child is fine." Gaby winces at her own words. "Well, as well as you can be, if that's how you died. I'm just glad you managed to climb out. Or..." Her face darkens slightly. "Or rather that you had some help yourself. It looked rather awkward the way you fell onto the pavement."

Her grimace makes me chuckle weakly. "I'm sure it looked as stupid as I feel now. But yes, Gaspar saved my life."

"Good man. You should keep him around."

If only. My heart aches at the bitter thought and I sigh. "I wonder where he is now."

"Isn't he here?" Gaby asks, sounding a little disappointed. "I thought I'd be able to thank him."

I look out the window again, but there's no sign of him. "That'll have to wait for another time, I guess." Annoyed at myself, I glance down at my bare ankles under the coat. "Well, that was a bust."

"We'll try again, but first we'll get you a taxi home. You need a warm shower and some proper dry clothes. And I need some, too."

What would I do without Gaby? "Then let's get going."

I don't like not knowing where Gaspar has gone all of a sudden, but it won't help either of us if I die of hypothermia now. With one last look at the grey tide, I follow Gaby outside.

CHAPTER 22

As it turns out, Gaspar had a very good reason for leaving me. I realise this when I hear a small child crying from my room. "What is it?" Gaby hisses at me in a whisper.

"I…"

To confirm my suspicion, I race into my room and close the door as soon as Gaby has slipped in. Gaspar is sitting on my desk chair, frantically bouncing a little girl with short braids on his knees. I recognise her immediately from my childhood photos and from a sudden pain in my heart.

"You found her," I whisper.

Gaby twists my arm until I gasp. "What's going on?"

"Um. Gaspar. He's found my spirit. She's here." My brain can't seem to process all of this at once. "I have to deal with this."

This time Gaby lets me do my thing without demanding a play-by-play. I approach my own desk cautiously, as if a poisonous snake rather than a distraught toddler ghost were waiting for me.

Gaspar looks up at me pleadingly. "It took me a while to convince her that I was taking her home, but then she saw your maman and... well, your maman didn't see her."

"Oh, sweetie." In a corner of my mind, I know I'm practically talking to myself here—more than usual—but all I see is a heart-broken little girl in desperate need of comfort. It hasn't quite sunk in yet that this is me. "Would you like a hug?"

Little Alix hides her face in Gaspar's hoodie. Apparently, she prefers him to me, which is fair enough, I suppose. I would too.

But she's still crying. I can't make my mother comfort someone she can't see, so I have to find something else to distract her. My eyes fall on Malou.

It's a bit early for her, but maybe that's a good thing. I walk over to her cage and gently lift the little hedgehog out before carrying her over to Gaspar.

"Hey, Petit Alix." Okay, that sounds a bit weird. Nevertheless, I continue. "Do you like hedgehogs?"

It works. Curiosity wins out over distress. She turns her tear-stained face towards me, leans into Gaspar, who has his arm around her shoulders protectively, and looks at Malou. After a while she nods.

"They're really cute, aren't they?" I lift Malou a little higher. "This is Malou. She's very sleepy right now, but you can touch her if you like. Don't worry, the spikes don't hurt."

Tentatively, Petit Alix stretches out a hand. Her first attempt is short-lived as she is startled by the sensation of the spikes. But then she tries again, and this time she cups her hand carefully to stroke Malou's spikes. Tears are still streaming down her face, but her eyes are wide open and she's smiling. "It feels prickly."

"It does." Seeing her take such good care of Malou warms my heart. "But she's really soft underneath." I carefully take one of my hands away and invite my younger self to give me hers.

When she tentatively touches my skin, I feel a jolt go through me. For a moment, I'm overwhelmed by feelings of abandonment that aren't mine. Meanwhile, Petit Alix seems calmer than ever as she reaches for Malou again, running her fingers over the soft fur on her belly.

A giggle bursts from her lips and the weight of those old, crusty feelings lifts. "She's really soft," she confirms. "Can I hold her?"

Normally I wouldn't trust a ghost to hold Malou, but my hedgehog's own ghost-sniffing abilities are enough for her to touch Gaspar, and whisper ghosts are said to be even stronger. So, with my hands ready to catch Malou, I gently pass her into the child's much smaller hands.

Petit Alix is now completely absorbed in Malou, taking great care not to let her fall. I breathe a sigh of relief and look up at

Gaspar, who's making sure they're both safe. Just like he made sure I was safe. My heart suddenly overflows with love, followed by a sharp pang of sorrow.

"How are you?" Gaspar whispers. He must have noticed the change in my emotions.

"I'm alright. I should probably take a shower."

"Go on," he urges. "I'll take care of her."

He seems to have everything under control, and that's probably for the best. A ghost can look after my ghostly self. And I need to look after myself.

After Gaby and I have both showered and changed into warm dry clothes, the four of us sit down on the bed; Gaby on my left and Gaspar with my mini me on my right. Malou has woken up and is climbing all over Petit Alix, trying to make sense of the new smell. Alix herself is squealing and giggling, happy for the moment. One day I'll have to sit down with her and explore these big feelings that have been her whole world for twenty years, but for now we both deserve a little break.

"So, what are you going to do with her now?" Gaby asks. "You can't keep a toddler in your room."

"Where else am I going to keep her?" I'm not saying Gaby isn't right, but I can hardly abandon Petit Alix on the street again. "She has no one to take care of her."

Gaby sighs heavily. "This is getting really confusing."

I lay my head on her shoulder in sympathy. "I know. I just wish you could see her too." My life would be so much easier if everyone was familiar with ghosts. But I guess easy wasn't in the job description.

"Does she have needs?" Gaby asks. "Like do you need to change her nappy or make sure she goes to bed early?"

"She doesn't need to sleep," Gaspar adds helpfully. "Or eat or drink. That's all in the past."

I relay his answer to Gaby and add: "She doesn't have any physical needs, only emotional ones. Remember, it's her spirit that goes on, not her body."

"Your spirit," Gaby points out and huffs at the surrealism of it all. "What is that like for you? Seeing yourself? Caring for yourself in the literal sense?"

"Weird. I haven't really grasped that she's me. I mean, theoretically I know that, and she looks exactly like me when I was younger, but it's still just a random kid." That's not quite true. My heart is hers, and we share a bond that I don't quite understand yet, but which is also unbreakable. Hardly a random child.

"Well, at least you've found her now." Gaby nudges me. "You should call Sébastien."

I suppose I should. Something inside me doesn't want to tell him yet, but it's the only thing that makes sense. Sébastien can guide me through the connection with Petit Alix and tell me what to do next, so I take out my phone and search for his number.

Just as my finger hovers over the phone symbol, someone knocks on my door. "Yes?"

As the door opens, Petit Alix lets out a squeal. "Papa!" Malou lands on the bed as my younger self slips off and runs towards my father, who sees through her to me.

"Hey girls. How are you, Gaby?" He completely ignores the little girl clinging to his legs.

"I'm fine. Thanks."

My father smiles vaguely before fixing his gaze on me. "Are you having a sleepover? Because if not, we could do the catacombs thing. Or, hey, Gaby's probably joining us, right?"

"Oh, no." Gaby shakes her head quickly. "I'll leave the amazing discovery to Alix. She's the one who found Molay."

"Gaby is claustrophobic," I explain.

"Ah, that's a shame. You're missing out, girl." My father chuck-les. "Well, look. I'm free today, tomorrow, and probably the day after that. So if you want, I think I can get us all packed up in an hour or so. It'd be fun to have another look around the old stomping grounds. See what's changed, watch my daughter make a groundbreaking discovery." He grins.

Gaby laughs too. "That sounds great. You two go and do that. I'll continue to scour the scientific papers for all the clues and evidence."

"One hour then," I agree and watch my father leave.

"Papa!" Petit Alix cries in a heartbreaking voice. "Why doesn't he look at me?"

Gaspar and I both hasten to kneel down in front of the little girl. "You know, things have changed a lot." How do I tell a toddler that she's dead?

"Come here, little one." Gaspar opens his arms. "I'll look at you."

Petit Alix throws herself into his arms and sobs again.

Over her shoulders, Gaspar says: "You go with your father. I'll take care of the little one."

"Are you sure?" After all, Gaspar is in his early twenties and probably hasn't planned on taking care of small children, let alone heartbroken ones, any time soon. Still, my little self is reassured by his presence.

"Yes. Just be careful down there. Stay away from the Crossroad of the Dead and avoid the Chevalier."

"I will."

By now Gaby must have guessed what happened on the floor. "Are you going to call Sébastien now?"

"Not now. I'll do it when I get back from the catacombs." It seems that Petit Alix will be well looked after in Gaspar's arms.

Involving Sébastien now will only complicate things. Better to take things one step at a time.

CHAPTER 23

Papa and I take the exact same route Emily showed me. I'm quite proud of myself for remembering where to turn and finding the little windows that lead us past the Crossroad of the Dead. It's also surprisingly fun to do this with my father. He has a dozen little stories about his adventures as a young man that I've never heard before, and he seems to thrive in this spooky atmosphere.

When we reach the small room with the glowing art installation, I make us stop and look at the ceiling. It's just as beautiful and soothing as the first time.

"Ah, this reminds me of the neon stars I once tried to put on this old bunker," my father muses.

"Neon stars?"

"Oh, you know the ones. A friend of mine helped me transform the bunker for a special surprise for your maman. I wanted to propose to her, but the damn stars kept falling down. It was a mess, and I was so upset I called the whole thing off."

"I thought you proposed at a picnic on the Buttes Chaumont." That's the story I've always heard.

My father nods wisely. "I did, but that was the backup plan, and I always kind of resented that. Not that I asked your mother, or that she took my sorry ass, but I really wanted the catacombs to be the place. Oh well, if I'd known about this place, I would have brought her here."

"It might not have been here yet."

"True."

We stare at the 'stars' for a little longer before having a snack and continuing on to the Boutique. I consult the piece of map the Chevalier once gave me to find our way, while my father continues the conversation.

"So how did you get down here?"

"Gaspar took me to a rave. And I fell more in love with the old tunnels than with the loud music." Both had been equally nice because Gaspar had been there. And both had ended with far more excitement than I'd been able to handle.

My father nods thoughtfully. "A classic move."

"Well, it worked for you and Maman."

He puts an arm around me and pulls me close. "You'll find someone who's worth all the growing pains."

"Growing pains?"

"You know, failed relationships, where you just find out who you really are and what you want. Or what you don't want. You grow up and find the one you can imagine a future with. Or you meet the person who will grow with you."

I don't answer, thinking about how I can imagine a future with Gaspar as much as I want. It won't happen. But he's perfect in just about every other way. He'd even have made a good father. The way he looks after my little ghost self proves that.

"Hey, don't make that face." My father pulls me close again. "It's going to be alright. Believe me."

For a moment I consider confiding in him. My father seems like he'd be more understanding. At least at the moment, but I'm afraid he'll react like Hélène and Maman. If he finds out about the ghosts now, it could jeopardise the story I'm trying to build for Molay. Above all, I need him to be my journalist father. That's the only way this is going to work.

"I know. And besides, I have more important things to do."

"Like finding the bones of Jacques de Molay," says Papa with some excitement. A last embrace follows. "My little girl will make quite a splash if this works out."

"We'll see."

For the next few hours, all we talk about is Jacques de Molay, the Knights Templar and all the interesting facts I've found out, but also how long it will probably take for everything to be verified and properly accepted by the scientific community. It's an interesting

process and we're only at the beginning of it, although I've managed to get a few steps ahead with my ghost-whispering skills. Even
if I don't succeed in getting his bones into the Panthéon, it will be
of great interest. The history of the Templars will be revisited, and
I'm sure he'll get some sort of monument.

We haven't nearly exhausted the subject by the time we reach
the Boutique. I show my father how to enter through the window,
then hold my breath as I remember how Ossa Arida was cleared
out before I could show it to Sébastien.

Fortunately, the Boutique of Psychosis didn't suffer the same
fate, and everything is exactly as it was. Even the ghosts are here,
lounging around as if it were the most exquisite gentlemen's club
in the world. I ignore them for my father's sake and show him
Molay's skeleton instead.

"See how the bones are charred? That's from the fire." I try not
to look at Molay himself, who approaches with a huge frown.

"What's the meaning of this?"

Again, I ignore him, though I try to gesture behind my father's
back to show him that he must trust me.

My father lowers his rucksack, completely mesmerised by my
find. "This is amazing." He hands me his torch and takes out
his camera. "Stand here and lift it up a bit." When I do as he
says, he moves closer and starts taking pictures. "Even if this isn't
Molay, as you say, it's an amazing find. We could do a story on

this arrangement alone. Do you know why the bones are chained together? I mean, this is clearly intentional. Spooky."

In fact, I don't know who was responsible for setting up Molay's skeleton in this way. I add it to the list of questions I have for the Grand Master that will hopefully lead me to the surviving evidence of what happened here.

"Where do the stairs lead to?" My father asks as he circles the column and discovers the spiral staircase leading to an upper level. "They can't be more than thirty, forty years old. Maybe eighty, if it comes to that."

I had almost forgotten about the stairs in the Boutique of Psychosis. Suddenly I remember someone coming down from above and following me. I'm half convinced much of what I experienced that night was a demonstration of Molay's power. He was trying to chase me out of the Boutique, so I can't be sure if there really was anyone there.

My hands itch as I fight the urge to just ask Molay. All I can do is give him a sharp look. Meanwhile, my father climbs the stairs, only to find the top blocked by a trapdoor. "It could be like the Palais Garnier. They still have an entrance to the catacombs. You know, the secret lake at the opera?"

"I know." Not that I'd thought to explore that particular part.

"What are you doing?" Molay hisses. "Who is this man?"

Since I can't answer him directly, I have to find a more indirect way. "Papa?"

"Yes, darling?"

"What do you need for the story on Molay? Just a few pictures?"

The Grand Master grimaces in disgust. "A story? My life and deeds are no story."

"Oh no, I'll need a lot of photographs. I wish the lighting was better. Is there anything you need to do? You probably can't take a bone."

"No, the historical society would have my head if I contaminated the material. It would all have to be documented and treated with the right equipment. And once we've managed to prove that the bones really do belong to Jacques de Molay, I bet there'll be a lot of public interest. He might even be buried in the Panthéon." Admittedly, that was a bit clumsy, but it contained all the important information.

"And so, we come full circle," says Papa wisely.

Molay is not amused. "That's your plan?" he thunders. "You're going to let the public decide my fate? Those stupid, gullible peasants?"

"Times have changed," I say, before realising that I'm not supposed to talk to ghosts.

Predictably, my father cocks his head. "Changed how?"

"Ugh, I mean in research. It's not like a hundred years ago or so, when you could just walk into a..."

"It'll be *years* before anything happens," Molay hisses, making me jump. "*If* anything happens at all."

Papa comes closer, frowning a little. "Are you alright, Alix?"

I start to panic. I know that Molay won't back down and doesn't care how it looks to my father. Meanwhile, my father is too smart to fall for a distraction. I can see the glint in his eye that always comes when he's on the verge of a breakthrough.

"What is it? You look like you've seen a ghost."

I almost laugh, because there are at least seven ghosts here, although only one is currently right in my face.

"It would be great if we could get a quick turnaround on this," I try to say, struggling to find a way to slip in a hidden message for Molay without sounding completely insane. "But I suppose it's been around for centuries, so a year or more won't matter."

"You promised to get me this audience now," Molay growls. "We had a deal."

Sweat breaks out on my skin as I remember how easily the Grand Master got into my head the last time. I didn't just promise to do him a favour. I did it in exchange for guaranteed safety. "This is the best way. A permanent—"

"Don't mess with me!" Molay thunders at me.

I can't help it. My body reacts to the hidden threat, and I jump backwards, my focus now on the ghost. "I'm trying!"

"Alix." The word cuts through the room like a whip. My father rushes to my side. "What's going on?"

"Papa, I..." Panic causes my head to dart between the two men demanding my attention. "It's nothing, I just..."

His concern cuts me off. "There's obviously something wrong. You're shaking and panting like you just ran a marathon."

"Tell him to leave," Molay orders. "We have things to discuss."

"I can't. Damn it!" It's only getting worse. "I'm sorry, Papa." Tears sting my eyes as I realise I'm going to have to explain everything to him now.

Papa strokes my cheek. "What are you sorry for?" He rests his forehead on mine. "Alix, you're driving me crazy. What's wrong with you? What's—"

He suddenly stops talking. There are things going on in his eyes that scare me to death. "Papa?"

Suddenly a hand falls on my shoulder and yanks me brutally away. Papa just stands there, staring into space, while Molay swings me around and slams me into the column. My head hits one of the stones and a sharp pain erupts. Pointed bones stab into my skin.

Jacques de Molay lowers his face until he's eye-to-eye with me, and I suddenly realise how much bigger and stronger—and more skilled with a weapon—this ghost is.

His voice is a gravelly threat delivered straight to my stomach. "Now, let's talk."

CHAPTER 24

In twenty years of dealing with ghosts, I've never been attacked by one. It never even occurred to me that they could do that, although it seems so obvious now. If a ghost can save my life, another can take it.

"Talk?" I whisper. My eyes are blurred from the pain in my head. I listen for my father, who would surely come running to my aid even if he couldn't see what was happening, but there is no other sound in the Boutique. "What have you done to my papa?"

"Nothing. Yet." The threat is undeniable and makes me whimper. "You broke our promise."

"I didn't!" I cry out. "Truly. The ghosts of the Panthéon won't let you in. They say you don't belong. But that won't matter when you're officially buried there. That's why I'm doing this. And it *can* work."

Molay creeps closer, pinning me between his body and the column. The bones behind me dig into my back, while the hidden chainmail under the white cloth cuts into my front. It doesn't matter that it's not real for anyone else. It'll be real to me. "'Can' isn't enough," he hisses. "And what do you mean, I don't belong?"

I have trouble breathing. "Just... Victor said..." My head is spinning. This sudden aggression confuses me. I was helping him. Somehow, I have to make Molay see it. "*I* think you belong."

"And yet you can't convince your upstart friend. Useless." He hisses the last word in my ear, increasing the pressure.

Useless. That's how I feel right now. "Please."

"Listen, little ghost whisperer. This is what we're going to do next."

I never get to hear what we're going to do next, because someone fires a bullet straight into Molay's head. Even though he's long dead and there's no wound to speak of, he stumbles backwards, bewildered. The man who shot him grabs my arm and pulls me out of Molay's trap. It's only when he pushes me behind him that I recognise him.

"Dix?"

"Get out of here! Now!" He sounds so much like Sébastien right now. I expect the GoPol agent to show his face too, but it's only his whisper ghost.

Molay has recovered from whatever it was that confused him and is now drawing a massive broadsword. My heart leaps into my throat as I watch his gaze settle on Dix. "You dare attack me, boy?"

Dix raises his weapon, which looks eerily like a real one, though he can't possibly have access to it. He points it at Molay's face with admirable coldness. "Oh, I dare much." From the corner of his mouth he whispers: "Go, Alix. You're not dead like us."

A chill runs through my veins and I back away carefully until I hit the wall with the window. I feel for the window with my fingers behind my back, not daring to take my eyes off the fight.

The Grand Master has raised his sword in front of his face, as if to shield himself from the bullets. Instead, he begins to whisper in Latin. His voice is too low for me to make out the meaning, but my body responds in its own way. Suddenly, the Boutique goes dark, as if a sinister presence has smothered the light. The other ghosts have retreated, but there's a whisper in the walls that makes me want to run away screaming.

I duck and put a foot through the window when I notice something. "Papa!"

My father is still in the room. He's been so quiet I thought he'd left, but he's standing where I last saw him, looking as if he'd been told to wait and never picked up. His eyes are staring into the void and his lips are moving without a sound.

I jump up again, but Dix has anticipated my move and pushes me back down. "Go!"

"I can't!" There's no way I can leave my father incapacitated in a room that's supposed to give people psychoses.

Jacques de Molay's lips curl. He must have realised the same thing. I tell myself that my father is safe. The ghost can't touch him, not the way he can touch me, but then the shadows in the room start to move, wrapping themselves around my father's chest and neck.

"Don't," I whimper, struggling to make sense of what I'm seeing. It goes against everything I thought I knew. I don't realise I'm trying to reach my father until Dix throws his arm around me and pulls me back. "Let me go!"

"No fucking way! Let's go while he's distracted."

"No!" I struggle against his grip, but he's bigger and stronger than me, even as a teenager.

The shadows around my father tighten, and he gasps. At last, he moves. But it's not to fight against this dark magic, or whatever it is, but to walk towards the column.

I kick and scream at Dix to let me go, while he whirls me around, away from my father. Throwing my head over the shoulder, I try to see what's happening. "Let me go, Dix!"

My father is now facing me, his back to Molay's skeleton. A shadow rises from the chains around the old bones and wraps itself around my father's torso, his hips, and his legs until he's bound to the column in a frightening mirror image of the dead man in front of him.

Ice is running through my veins. My entire body goes rigid, which makes it both harder and easier for Dix to manoeuvre me towards the window. My knees land on the stone floor, but even the pain doesn't manage to jolt me out of my shock.

Grand Master Molay has abandoned his sword and presses his palm onto my father's forehead. Again, he speaks in Latin, and this time I pick up the name of the devil and some sort of promise. When he lets go of my father again, a dark symbol has etched itself into his skin. Papa closes his eyes as if he's in pain.

"Papa!"

Molay's gaze hits me. "I want that audience."

That's all he manages to say before Dix pushes my head through the window. Or perhaps it's all he wants to say, since the consequences have been made abundantly clear. He's letting me go, and though I don't want to, there's no fighting the whisper ghost who shoves me out of the Boutique and into the dark tunnels behind it.

The weight on my heart lifts as soon as we step out of the damned room. It's easier to breathe, but the panic doesn't leave me. "We need to go back."

Dix pulls me to my feet and continues to ignore what I'm saying. "That's not going to happen, stupid."

"I'm not stupid. That's my papa in there."

Annoyed, he tugs at my arm, making me stumble into him. "And that could be *you* if I don't get you out of here."

"What are you even doing here?" I'm not exactly complaining that he's here, but it's just occured to me again that he's alone, no ghost whisperer agent in sight.

"Making sure you don't get into trouble, though that seems to be impossible." He says it as if it's somehow my fault a crazy ghost, who apparently *is* a devil worshipper attacked me. "What were you thinking going in there?"

"I—"

A light blinds me all of a sudden. My heart jumps straight back into my throat, and I blink furiously, until slowly, a figure becomes visible against the brightness. Before I can take a closer look, Dix puts himself in between me and the new arrival. "Get back!" he bellows.

"Is that your ghost?" a familiar voice asks, sending further chills down my back.

We're no safer outside the Boutique of Psychosis than we were inside of it, because le Chevalier d'Os has found me.

Chapter 25

"I'm sensing a strong repulsive energy," the Chevalier explains, as if I'm not about to pee myself with fear. "There must be a whisper ghost."

"I'll show him repulsive energy!" Dix says, raising his ghostly weapon.

Panic grips me and I lunge for his arm. "Don't!"

Annoyed, he shakes me off. "It won't kill him."

The Chevalier seems amused by my antics. I probably look hilarious. "I didn't mean to scare you, Alix."

Breathing heavily, I take a step back, but not more, for that would bring me too close to the Boutique of Psychosis. "What do you want from me?" I swear, I'll scream if he tries to recruit me again.

But the Chevalier shakes his head. "Nothing. I didn't even know you were here until I saw you in the tunnel. I sensed something going on in the Boutique and came to check it out. You sensed it too, didn't you? Now you know why I need this room cleared."

Slowly, my panic fades, allowing me to think more clearly. "You knew about Molay?"

"Is that the ghost's name?" the Chevalier asks. "I never really found out who he was, only that he's very old and powerful, probably even more powerful than when he was alive, having drunk the power of the Boutique. Or perhaps the Boutique became so powerful because of him."

Fragmented memories come back to me. Something about places of power and the Chevalier's search for them. Perhaps I was wrong about him from the start. He's always wanted to rid this place of the ghosts, that's why he sent me here in the first place. To make the catacombs safe from ghosts like Molay.

I decide to trust him with a little information. "His name is Jacques de Molay. He was the last Grand Master of the Knights Templar, burned at the stake for..." I swallow hard. "Blasphemy, idolatry, and devil worship."

The Chevalier's eyes widen. "That explains so much."

"You think it's real? That there's a devil giving Molay power?"

"There is something." He makes an inviting gesture. "Come, let's go somewhere safer where we can compare notes and make a proper plan."

Dix puts his hand on my wrist. "Don't trust him."

I don't know who to trust anymore. The Chevalier has still very likely murdered someone and chased me with a gun, whether he intended to shoot me or not. Apparently, ghost guns are a thing. I can't really trust Dix either, although he at least seems to have my back, but he shouldn't even be here. And I certainly can't trust Molay, who flipped the switch and went all psycho on me. Besides, he's got my papa in custody.

Right now, the only one who could really help me is the one I fear the most. "I can't go anywhere," I tell the Chevalier. "Look, I came here with my father. He's still in the shop. Molay has done something to him, something dark and sinister. Papa can neither move nor see nor hear. He's in a kind of trance, and now he's been marked with... I don't know, a devil's mark."

Concern immediately washes over the Chevalier's face. "This is no good. This isn't good at all." He walks towards me as if to charge straight into the Boutique, but Dix pushes him back. And though the whisper ghost can't touch him the way he can touch me, there's enough charge in the air to make the Chevalier hesitate. He looks at the dark window, then at me. "You know the stories about the Boutique?"

"The ones you kept from me when you first sent me there?"

The Chevalier gives me a rueful look. "I'm sorry. I thought you were my chance to get rid of them once and for all. But it seems we both underestimated what's going on in there."

The need to ask him more about this is so strong it hurts, but I can't be distracted. "I have to save my father."

Dix stomps his foot. "We can't. You're no match for him, and neither am I. You can't kill a ghost once you've noticed it." But his strategic mind doesn't stop there. "I might be able to repel him enough for you to reach your father, but I don't know if you'll be able to free him, and if he starts those weird incantations again, I won't be much help." He seems to really hate the thought.

"What does Molay want from you?" the Chevalier asks, deaf to Dix's strategising.

It's so hard to stay calm and think, when all I want to do is jump back in and fight tooth and nail for my father's sanity. "He wants an audience with the ghosts of the Panthéon. They've refused him time and again. I had a plan to get his bones discovered and eventually transferred to the Panthéon, but apparently that's not good enough." My voice thickens as tears well up in my eyes. All that research and careful planning, only to be betrayed like this. And on top of that, I got my father into ghost trouble.

Shaking, I take a deep breath before continuing. "He wants me to go back up there and convince them." I don't see how that's going to work. Victor seemed adamant that he wouldn't grant this audience. And I'm a little afraid that this meeting Molay wants is the beginning of something sinister, not the innocent talk I originally thought.

"Alright, this is what we're going to do," the Chevalier announces. Apparently there's a "we" now. "You go back upstairs and try your best to do what he wants. If you succeed, great, it'll buy us more time, but if not, don't worry. We'll meet back at the Crossroad tomorrow at midnight to barge back in."

"How will that change anything?" Dix asks, disgusted by what he's heard so far.

I don't interrupt the Chevalier to ask his question, but I'm dying to know the answer.

"Meanwhile, I'll gather everything we need to kill a ghost."

"Kill a ghost?" Dix asks outraged, and this time I echo his words.

The Chevalier gives me a wry grin. "I'm nothing if not resourceful. You're not as invincible as you think. Especially when you have access to their bones."

"Well, there's no chance of him getting Séb's bones," Dix says grumpily.

I would have laughed if the situation wasn't so serious. Instead, I put my hand on Dix's arm. "He doesn't want to kill you."

The Chevalier's eyes narrow, and it almost seems as if he can see Dix. "Of course I won't kill your whisper ghost. That's the last thing I want to do."

"He's not mine," I say finally. "Although I have no idea where his whisperer is."

Dix grimaces. "Sleeping. Like living people do. He asked me to keep an eye on you because he was afraid you'd go against his advice. As you obviously have." When I look at him indignantly, Dix grins. "Don't worry, I'd have done the same in your position."

"I can't believe Sébastien would have me followed."

The Chevalier seems to understand that I'm talking to a ghost much better than anyone else ever has. "Roubert junior?" he asks. "I could have told you." He looks at the empty space where he thinks Dix is. "But perhaps we could use GoPol's expertise to our advantage. Do you agree with my plan?"

It hurts my heart to even think about leaving my father down here. I still want to go back in, but I've calmed down enough to know it's a stupid idea. One that will only get me killed—or worse.

Since I don't know anything about battle plans, I look at Dix. The whisper ghost doesn't look too happy, but in the end he nods. "If he can really kill a ghost like that, we should try it."

I turn back to the Chevalier. "We're in."

CHAPTER 26

Dix insists on bringing me back to the surface, not leaving my side until the opening is right in front of us. It's still dark outside and my phone tells me it's only four in the morning. The Panthéon doesn't open until ten. Not that I care about opening hours.

"You can go now," I say, my voice thin with exhaustion. "Unless you need to watch me."

"Are you planning to turn around and run back in the moment I leave?"

My brain takes far too long to understand why I should. "No. I..."

"Then you don't need to be watched." Dix grins. When he notices that I'm not laughing with him, he sighs. "Maybe you should sit this one out. Let the Chevalier and Sébastien deal with Molay."

"That's my father in there," I remind him. There's no way I'm going to stay home while they risk their lives and their sanity to clean up my mess.

"So?"

I stare at him in confusion until it dawns on me that Dix holds some kind of grudge against his own father. "I love my father."

He raises an eyebrow, then shrugs. "I see. But let's be honest. If you can't get those old crooks at the Panthéon to grant Molay his damned audience, you won't be much help. So, emotions aside, why don't you leave it to the experts?"

"You mean the men?"

Outraged, Dix shakes his head. "No, what I mean is that you have no training for this sort of thing and you're still fairly new to the catacombs. What do you bring to the table that makes it worth the risk?"

"I know Molay." I try not to be offended by his assessment. The truth is that I'm only a history student. Facts and obscure knowledge are all I've got. I wasn't trained as a special agent from the moment I could walk, and I'm not an expert in catacombs crawling like the Chevalier. But that doesn't mean I'm useless. "The Grand Master made a deal with me. And now that I know the whole story—or at least a lot more than I did before—I may be able to use it against him. At least I can distract him while you take him down."

Dix opens his mouth to protest, but then reconsiders and nods. "That's actually a workable plan. In that case, I'll see you here tomorrow at six, History Girl."

History Girl? I'll take that.

With a wink, Dix disappears in front of me. I can only hope he's really gone and not following me invisibly. Bringing him with me to the Panthéon would only create drama, for which I have no patience today. Even without Dix, I have little hope of changing the ghosts' minds. I've already used my friendship to let Gaspar in. If only he were here.

I'm about five metres from the entrance when I see him coming towards me. I don't know if he's always wanted to be here or if I've just summoned him, but I throw myself at him as soon as he steps into my light. "It's all gone to shit!" I may have played it hard for Dix, but I'm a complete mess.

"Alix." He wraps his arms around me and hugs me tightly. His left hand is buried in my hair as he presses my face into his shoulder and whispers in my ear, "Shh, it's going to be okay."

"No, no, it won't." The wave of emotion I thought I'd overcome after the Chevalier, Dix, and I came up with a plan comes crashing down on me mercilessly.

"What happened?"

In bits and pieces, I tell Gaspar what happened down at the Boutique of Psychosis, how Molay betrayed me, and how he's holding my father's mind as a bargaining chip. When I get to the plan I made with Dix and the Chevalier, I calm down again. "We'll go back in tomorrow, but our chances are much better if I can get the Panthéon to meet with Molay."

Gaspar takes my hand and nods with a sombre expression. "Let's go and do that then."

I'm glad he doesn't suggest I get some sleep first, because I'll never get any with all these thoughts and fears swirling around my head. At this time of night, it'll be much easier to talk to the ghosts of the Panthéon. No nosy tourists or workmates to worry about.

"What about Petit Alix?" I ask, sparing a thought for what stopped Gaspar from coming with me in the first place.

"She's settled in very well. Malou's keeping her company, and the presence of your mother seems to be quite reassuring now she's accepted your mother won't react to her." Gaspar looks a little pained as he looks at me. "If you want me to go back, let me know, but I really think she'll be fine on her own for a few hours."

He doesn't have to say it. Petit Alix has been on her own for twenty years.

"Honestly, I could use a friend right now." I slip my hand into his. "As soon as this is over, I'll talk to Sébastien, and we'll find a permanent solution. I don't expect you to babysit my whisper ghost." That wouldn't be right.

"I don't mind." Gaspar tugs at my hand and smiles gently. "Do you think I would have walked past a crying child when I was alive?"

No. I might not have known him then, but the Gaspar I've met wouldn't. He's not just doing me a favour. He really cares. "Thank you."

"Of course. Any time. Now let's talk to those ghosts of yours."

CHAPTER 27

I use the spare key to open the side entrance, and lock behind me as soon as Gaspar has entered. I don't bother with the lights as I don't want to draw attention to the Panthéon. The last thing I need today is a police interrogation.

It takes a moment for the ghosts to realise that my presence at this time of night is out of the ordinary. I make it halfway to the crypt when Jean Lannes de Montebello, who served in the Revolutionary and Napoleonic Wars, approaches me. "You're too early for work." He's one of the many officers who guard the Panthéon.

"I'm not working today," I tell him.

He frowns deeply. "Is the city burning?"

"The city above is fine. The catacombs, not so much." A bit dramatic, but it seems to fit the gravity of what has happened tonight.

I don't know how Jean does it, but by the time my feet touch the floor of the crypt, the rest of the ghosts are flocking to me. Even Marie Curie stops her experiments and brings her eerie glow with her. I take a cautious step back and stay close to the stairs.

Victor pushes his way to the front of the exalted group. "What happened?"

Gaspar squeezes my hand, giving me the courage to face all these lovely but intimidating men and women. "You must make an exception for Jacques de Molay and grant him an audience."

Disappointment washes over Victor's face. Others are more vocal. "Absolutely not! No more exceptions. This is our place. We're the chosen ones."

"Chosen for what?" Gaspar asks, obviously offended at being the dreaded exception.

Voltaire ignores him and turns to me. "If you think you have any power over us just because you work here, I'm sorry to tell you that's not the case. Just because you're alive doesn't mean you get to dictate what we do."

"Leave the girl alone," Josephine Baker rudely interrupts. "She's not dictating anything. She's asking."

"Please. Molay has…" I take a deep breath. "Molay has my father. He's holding him hostage as we speak. Please, if you care about me at all, grant him this small audience."

"You have no idea," Voltaire mumbles under his breath, still angry with me. He glares at me for good measure. "No. The answer is no."

Jean-Jacques Rousseau clears his throat, and for a moment I'm hopeful—for once their bitter rivalry might work in my favour—but all he says is, "As much as I hate it, I have to agree with Voltaire on this. Molay does not belong here."

More and more ghosts are raising their voices against me. My head swims as I realise they're already voting. "My papa will lose his mind!" I shout at them. They may be dead, but my father isn't. And neither am I. "Please! It costs you nothing! Nothing!" I can't believe they won't even consider it for a minute.

The crowd begins to disperse, and I feel the panic rising in my throat. They haven't even listened to me. I thought these ghosts were my friends, and they don't even care. As if it only amused them to entertain me and my quirks. Bitterness fills my mouth and I have trouble swallowing. It all hurts too much.

"Wow!" Gaspar exclaims loudly. "Is that any way to treat a friend?" The ghosts stop, their glare hitting Gaspar. "Alix has given you everything! Ever since she started working here, you've been inundating her with requests. Small, petty requests like picking up the rubbish or correcting inconsequential details about your life. And not once has she batted an eyelid, instead going out of her way to help you. She took care of you, and this is how you repay her?"

When he says it like that, it's even more hurtful. At the same time, I melt a little, because even though we've only known each other for a short time, he's willing to go into battle for me.

"Molay does NOT belong here," Voltaire yells at me, getting right in my face. "And neither does *he*." He shakes his hand in Gaspar's direction. "This wannabe, never-been is not one of us. Letting ghosts like him in undermines everything this place stands for."

Gaspar crosses his arms and snorts. "This is bullshit. And to think people look up to the likes of you."

"Careful, boy," Alexandre Dumas warns. "Don't say anything you'll regret."

"I'm not afraid of you. I'm disappointed." Without a trace of fear, Gaspar takes another step into the crypt. He turns and looks at each of the famous figures before shaking his head. "You are supposed to be the men and women who shaped our country. The people we aspire to be. Men and women of the people. But you don't care about anyone but yourself. Your reputations. Your needs."

Voltaire is seething. If Rousseau hadn't held him back by his waistcoat, he would have throttled Gaspar by now. "Let the boy speak."

"There are millions of ghosts out there who don't have the same privileges as you, who fade away when their loved ones are gone, who hang on by the thinnest of threads and look up to you. And you ignore them. You refuse to speak to them, to listen to their concerns, to let even them bask in your presence for even a meagre minute. Some fine leaders you are, up here in your ivory tower. You lament the loss of your life, the loss of your influence, but you're too far up your own asses to see the difference you could make to the ghost community. Instead, you send Alix. A living girl whom you've already dismissed from your ranks. You don't value her; you don't value anyone but yourselves."

Gaspar spits at Voltaire's feet. "There, that's how much you're worth to anyone, dead or alive."

Voltaire explodes. He screams and yells, and a second later four soldiers descend on Gaspar and brutally drag him from the crypt.

"Gaspar!" Fear floods my mind. Are the ghosts going to destroy him? Does Voltaire have that kind of power? Have I lost Gaspar forever?

A heavy hand lands on my shoulder. Victor catches me just as my knees buckle. "He's fine, Alix. Voltaire has just thrown him out. He's been banned."

How is that fine? I want to ask, but the relief is almost as strong as the panic. Losing Gaspar has become unthinkable. It should frighten me how quickly I've become attached to him, but he's been the one bright spot in an otherwise momentous shit show. A shit show that my dearest ghost friends were happy to buy into.

I clench my fists. "No, he's not fine. A lot of people aren't alright."

"If you mean ghosts, let me remind you that we're dead. We're neither fine nor anything else. We simply exist," Victor instructs me.

"Actually," Rousseau interjects, "that's far too simple. Our afterlife has meaning. We—"

"Not now!" I bark. Slowly I get to my feet, shaking off Victor's helping hand. "Gaspar was right. I've heard every one of your philosophical theories."

Rousseau mumbles something about "hardly", but I ignore him.

"I made sure your resting places were clean and tended. I risked my job by changing what I'm supposed to say because I wanted to do right by you. I know I'm not your equal and never will be, but I thought you cared about me. My talents are wasted here. There are less fortunate spirits who need me more than you."

I won't wait for them to cast me out. They may not be able to ban me, but that won't stop the generals from trying. Instead, I turn on my heels and walk up the stairs, head held high. I'll probably regret quitting my job, but after tonight I can't imagine looking any of them in the eye again. Gaspar was right. The Panthéon is an ivory tower. You have more than enough admirers who don't talk back. They don't need a ghost whisperer like me.

Not everyone is happy to see me go. Some call after me, asking me to stay and reconsider, expressing their remorse. Some of the military ghosts salute me with sad faces. Rousseau loudly accuses

Voltaire of having ruined everything once again. But it wasn't just Voltaire. They all agreed with him. No one thought for a second to help me in my hour of need.

Gaspar is running circles on the steps of the Panthéon and lets out a huge sigh of relief when he sees me. He rushes to me and cups my face with his hands. "Are you alright? Did they hurt you?"

I huff. "Physically, no. Emotionally, different."

He immediately pulls me into a tight hug. "I'm so sorry. I shouldn't have blown up at them like that."

"No. Everything you said was right. I was just blinded by their notoriety to see what an exclusionary bunch they are."

"You're better than any of them," Gaspar says with endearing conviction. To him, I really am. "And we'll get your father back without their help. They can't do anything anyway, they just sit around and bask in their own greatness."

"The disrespect of today's youth is appalling."

I whirl around in shock. "Victor!"

Victor Hugo clears his throat before chuckling softly. But his eyes are filled with sorrow and regret. "I'm sorry we disappointed you tonight, Alix."

I cross my arms anxiously, steeling myself against his usual charm.

"It may seem we all think too highly of ourselves, and we probably do, but there's more at work here than that. Things I can't tell you about because, quite frankly, they're none of your business."

Victor cocks his head apologetically. "Let *us* deal with the ghost business."

"Right. I was good enough to handle ghost business when it suited you, but now I need to stay out of it."

He sighs deeply. "It would've been better, but I suppose, it's a little too late for that. The reason I warned you off against going into the catacombs is because I *do* care about you. There are dark things down there, which I guess, you've already encountered." Victor nods, suddenly having made up his mind. "We will not let Molay in. We cannot allow him to taint this place. You went behind our backs to force him on us."

My cheeks are flushing with heat. "How did you—?"

"I've got my connections. Contrary to what your young friend says, I don't just sit on my... ass." He grimaces as he speaks the word, as if it leaves a bad taste in his mouth. "I know what you were trying to do, and it hurt too, but I realise that it's a failing of my own making. I didn't give you a proper reason to trust my word. Nor did I realise the hold Molay already had on you when you first asked."

He smiles warmly at me. "You were out of your depth, and that's my fault. I didn't prepare you enough to make the right decisions."

I wince. Taking my father with me to see Molay was definitely a wrong decision. It came from the heart, though. "I just wanted to help."

"Yes, I know," Victor replies, his voice laced with remorse. "That's what you always do. And Gaspar is right, we owe you."

Does that mean there's hope after all? Cautiously, I ask. "Will you help?"

"Yes."

"You're going to grant Molay an audience?"

It seems to pain Victor greatly, but he nods at last. "I will. Not in the crypt. That can never happen. But I will meet with Molay, while you... Do you have a plan?"

Swallowing, I nod. "Yes. There is a plan." Do I dare tell him about the Chevalier's claim to know how to destroy a ghost for good? Victor might be able to tell me if that's even possible. In the end, I decide against it. I no longer trust him enough to have my back. "I'm going back in tomorrow... tonight."

Victor nods gravely. "I will summon Molay to me then."

My stubbornness streak gives a little. "Thank you."

CHAPTER 28

Through sheer exhaustion, I manage a few hours of irregular sleep. In my dreams, Jacques de Molay is waiting for me, his figure towering over me, his sword raised. But it's not his weapon that frightens me. It's the power the Boutique gives him to conjure up my greatest fears and drown me in nightmares.

I wake around four in the afternoon, having watched each and every one of my family and Gaby go mad. My heart is racing, my breath is ragged, and the sheets are soaked with sweat. A glance at the clock makes all that irrelevant. I jump under the shower and stuff some food into my mouth. My brain doesn't register the taste, it just knows it needs food.

With more than an hour to spare, I make my way to the entrance of the catacombs in the suburbs. There, a simple thought of Gaspar calls him to my side. "How are things at home?"

While I had sought refuge at Gaby's, Gaspar had returned home. I couldn't face my mother and Odile without revealing Papa's precarious condition. There's still time for that if I fail tonight. Not that that's an option.

"Everything is fine. Your maman doesn't suspect a thing, and your sister had a full-ass photo session with Malou?" Gaspar looks at me sceptically.

I roll my eyes. "It's for Instagram. Odi set up an account for Malou and is low-key obsessed with it."

"Well, the world can't have enough cute hedgehog pictures."

My hedgehog boy shines through and makes me smile as usual. "And Petit Alix?"

"Surprisingly well for her age, but she's lonely. She needs someone to look after her."

"When this is all over, I will." I have no idea how I'm going to manage a toddler ghost on top of my schoolwork, but now that I'm leaving the Panthéon, I should have more time than usual.

I still haven't forgiven the ghosts there, even though Victor came through at the last minute. I understand that the affairs of the living are irrelevant to them. Our short life spans are nothing compared to their eternal afterlife, but after believing in these supposed greats all my life, I was blindsided by their egocentrism.

It takes about half an hour for the others to arrive. Dix simply appeared, strolling along the muddy bank without ever getting his trainers dirty. He waves to me but seems to take offence at Gaspar's presence. "What's he doing here?"

Before Gaspar can answer, the roar of a motorbike gets louder. As it reaches its peak, the bike appears at the top of the embankment, its wheels spraying mud into the air as the rider slams on the brakes. Sébastien takes off his helmet and looks at us.

"Show-off," mutters Dix.

"Wouldn't that also make you a show-off?" Gaspar asks.

"Do you see me with a motorbike? When I died, we were still riding a stupid moped."

I suppose that rules out a motorcycle accident as the cause of death. We wait for Sébastien to come down the embankment. His helmet remains with his bike, but his riding gear seems to double as some sort of armour. He tosses me a surprisingly heavy bundle.

"What's this?" I ask as I straighten it out. It turns out to be some sort of vest.

"Minimal protection gear. The padding is designed to deflect glancing blows and stray bullets."

"Bullets?" I notice he's got a gun in his holster. "What's that for?"

He looks down. "Don't worry about it. It's for the ghosts."

"Ghosts can be killed with bullets?"

"If they're salt bullets. And no, it won't kill them, but it will keep them away for a fair while." Unlike Dix, Sébastien nods at

Gaspar. "You brought some reinforcements, good. Not as good as a whisper ghost, but he seems surprisingly stable."

"If that means I'll be loyal to Alix and keep her safe at all costs, then yes, damn."

I try not to swoon too much. As long as there are no real swords or bullets involved, I'll be safe with Gaspar.

I take off my jacket and put on the vest while Sébastien helps me adjust the fit. "There, that should do it."

"Where did you get one in my size?" I ask as I pull my jacket back on. It's obviously not his spare bulletproof vest I'm wearing.

"It's my partner's."

Surprised, I blink at him. "Your partner?"

"Ex-partner," Dix adds before Sébastien has the chance. "And not a romantic partner either. Just work."

Sébastien looks confused as to why Dix felt the need to add that distinction. "Either way. We had equipment stored at each other's places. You're about her size, so that saved me a trip to GoPol to get one."

"And we're all about saving trips to GoPol," Dix says with a mad grin, putting his arm around Sébastien's shoulder. "Right, Séb?"

Annoyed, Sébastien shakes off his younger self. "Speak for yourself." He checks his watch. "We've got about four hours if we want to meet le Chevalier d'Os at the Crossroad of the Dead."

I raise an eyebrow. "*If?*"

"I don't trust the guy." The look Sébastien gives me challenges me to contradict him.

"There's a good chance he's a murderer." Since ghosts aren't the most trustworthy of people, I can't put too much stock in Emily's words, especially after the shit she's already pulled on me. Still... "No, I don't trust him either."

Sébastien lets out a small breath of relief. "But you still want to work with him?"

Far from it, but I don't see what choice I have. I walk to the gate and grasp the bars beside the hole with both hands. "He knows how to destroy a ghost. Do you?"

When Sébastien doesn't answer, I pull myself through the gap in the gate. I'm not sure how I feel about the prospect of destroying Jacques de Molay, despite the fact he's holding my father hostage. It feels like a great sacrilege to wipe him from existence. He will still be remembered, of course, but he will cease to exist, and I don't like that. I tell myself that it's only a last resort; if we can't get my father back.

Gaspar and Sébastien climb in after me, while Dix just walks through the gate as if it were made of air. I suppose Gaspar will follow eventually, but for now, he hasn't changed his ways.

By now I know by heart how to get to the deeper levels of the catacombs, and I lead the pack at a fast pace. Sébastien catches up and falls into step beside me, while the two ghosts stay back.

"Thanks for coming." I know he doesn't have to. None of this has anything to do with GoPol.

"Of course." Sébastien seems offended that I'd even doubt him. "Dix told me what happened down there. Do you think I'd leave you alone with that? Alone with le Chevalier d'Os?" he adds with a sneer.

"I still don't know exactly what happened in the Boutique," I admit. "How can he have such power? Is it really devil worship?"

Sébastien raises an eyebrow. "Devil worship?"

"Jacques de Molay was tried and executed by the King for devil worship and idolatry. I've always been under the impression that these were just unfounded claims, defamation of a forgotten time, not the plain truth." I look at Sébastien nervously. "GoPol must know about these things, don't they?"

He pulls a face. "I don't believe in magic. And devil worship definitely falls into that category. But there is something."

"You could say that seeing ghosts is magic."

Sébastien gives me a half-smile. "But we both know that's not true."

"Do we?"

He shakes his head with a snort. "I suppose, if you want to get philosophical, it's just magic until you figure out how it works. You're the history student. Didn't people once believe that lightning was divine punishment?"

I know what he means. People used to explain all sorts of natural phenomena in terms of the supernatural, then dismissed them as superstition as our knowledge grew. Many still do. "That may be true, but then it's just a name, and the fact remains that Molay is far more powerful than ghosts should be. He used some sort of incantation to control the shadows in the room, and he was able to control my father, even though he's not a ghost whisperer like me."

Sébastien considers my words, then nods. "We'll have to think of something. The priority is to get your father back to the surface."

Slightly surprised that he would think of my father first, I stop in my tracks. "Not destroy Molay?"

He shakes his head. "As far as I am concerned, the ghosts can do whatever they want. Their business is of no interest to us. It's when they mess with the living that we step in. Your father is in trouble, and we'll do whatever it takes to get him out safely, but beyond that we're always told to stay out of ghost business. Maybe you should too," he adds as a gentle suggestion.

"How can you stay out of ghost business when you're involved with one?"

"You mean Dix? He's just an extension of me. A tool. He doesn't mix with other ghosts beyond the mission we serve."

I look back at Dix, who's walking with Gaspar and arguing passionately with him. They have just caught up with us. Immediately, Dix groans. "Alix, he's not going to be of any help. He's not even used to being dead yet. He's just a little boy without any experience."

"Who's the little boy here?" Gaspar asks, outraged.

Sébastien glares at Dix. "He's all Alix has for now. He'll have to do."

Frustrated, Gaspar falls in step on my other side and mumbles, "The sooner we get away from these wannabe superheroes, the better."

I link my arm with his and pat him on the shoulder. "You're more than enough for me."

The instant smile on his face almost makes me chuckle. On my other side, Sébastien frowns. Good. He needs to see that ghosts are more than just tools to be used, including Dix. From what I've seen, Dix didn't suddenly lose all his dreams and desires, his traumas, and fears when he died. If anything, he's more alive than the part that survived.

By now the Banga is no longer an obstacle. I set my feet on the subterranean path as safely as Gaspar once did, enduring the cold of the water for the length of the traverse. Down here in the catacombs, the temperature is a steady, comfortable fifteen degrees, much warmer than the chill outside.

After a short break for a snack and a drink, we continue on to the Crossroad of the Dead. It's the first time I've been here since my first fateful visit, and the sight still blows me away. If anything, there are even more ghosts walking around or chatting to each other.

"Huh," is all Sébastien says, and I figure he used to keep his distance from this place.

Meanwhile, Gaspar leans in to whisper, "There are so many ghosts here."

"I know. It surprised me too when I first came here. And you? It must have been very different from what you're used to." I remember how tense he was when we first came here together.

Gaspar swallows. "I saw them, of course, but it didn't add up. I guess I didn't want to understand."

I give him a quick squeeze of the hand, then pull him towards the steps that lead to the upper floor, the Chevalier's headquarters. "You're coming with me this time."

"Absolutely."

Meanwhile, Sébastien orders Dix: "Stand guard. We don't want to be ambushed."

Dix gives him a mock salute before taking up the same position Gaspar occupied last time. Despite his lax posture, his gaze is alert as he examines the ghosts around him.

Unlike last time, the upper floor is almost empty. I was expecting the Chevalier to meet us with a group of cataphiles, as I know for a fact he doesn't work alone, but directs a vast network, like a spider in its web. But none of them are here. Even the regular ghosts have cleared out. Instead, we find the Chevalier alone, poring over a map, a rucksack packed next to him.

As soon as he hears our footsteps, he looks up and grins. "Ah, there you are, Alix. And you brought your bodyguard with you." He nods at Sébastien. "Does your daddy know?"

"This isn't official GoPol business."

"I see." The Chevalier rolls up his map and waves me over. "Have you managed to persuade the ghosts of the Panthéon to hear Molay out?"

He pours us all coffee from a thermos and offers us biscuits. Sébastien refuses, but I'm glad of the caffeine boost after the little sleep I've had tonight.

"Not quite, but Victor Hugo will meet Molay at the time we should arrive at the Boutique. He'll distract him for us." *Long enough, I hope*, I add quietly.

The Chevalier whistles through his teeth. "*The* Victor Hugo does your bidding? I'm impressed."

"I wouldn't really call it *doing my bidding*." The Panthéon ghosts made it very clear that they wouldn't listen to anything I said. "But we've been friends for a few years, and he's agreed to help me as best he can." Only he could've done so much more. I'm still sore from that meeting, but the Chevalier doesn't need to know.

My relationship with ghosts is the only advantage I have among these experts. That, and my knowledge of their deeds.

"Do you know them all?" the Chevalier asks. "Voltaire? And who else? Zola? The Curies?"

I nod at each of them. "Yes. They don't all spend equal time with me, but I know every ghost in the Panthéon and many in the other necropolises."

"Impressive." For the first time, the Chevalier meets Sébastien's eyes. "Impressive, isn't she? No wonder you're courting her." As if we're best friends, the Chevalier bumps my elbow with his. "Don't believe his glorious GoPol stories. They're not as shiny as he makes them out to be."

Nothing Sébastien has told me about GoPol has seemed shiny. He also snorts. "I have no interest in recruiting them."

As I have no interest in joining GoPol, the comment doesn't even sting.

The Chevalier's smile fades. "That's what I thought," he says. "If you know what's good for you, Alix, stay away from them."

"The same could be said for you, but here I am." I don't need a pissing contest between the two of them when my father's sanity is at stake. "What's the plan? Victor distracts Molay, we get my father out, and leave before he comes back?"

"It won't work, sweetheart."

And now we're using infantilising terms. Yeah, I don't trust the Chevalier any more than I trust Sébastien. Much less, in fact. "It won't?"

"Look at this." He unfolds his map. The first thing I notice is how much bigger it is than the one he'd given me earlier. At first, I don't see it, but then I notice the pale silver lines that are the streets and squares of upper Paris. From what I can make out, it's a complete map of the catacombs.

Le Chevalier d'Os points to a blue spot on the map, the part I recognise: la Boutique de la Psychose. He then points to a number of similarly marked spots. Among them I recognise the cemeteries in Paris, St Denis, the royal tomb, Les Invalides with Napoleon, and the Panthéon. There are also several places in the catacombs that seem to have no obvious connection to the above, such as the Crossroad of the Dead itself.

"All these places you see here are places of power, where ghosts gather. Either a lot of them, or those with a powerful presence," the Chevalier explains freely, reiterating what Gaspar had found out earlier. "The Boutique is one of the most powerful. It has residual spiritual energy readings that are only surpassed by Les Invalides and the Panthéon. For a long time, I couldn't understand why. What kind of spirit gave it so much power? Until you came along."

The Chevalier straightens his back. "Jacques de Molay, the last Grand Master of the fabled Knights Templar. Hidden just below what used to be their stronghold."

I look at the map again and realise he's right. The Boutique is in the same place as the Square du Temple in the Marais. Figures. The only question is how his skeleton got there. But that's of historical interest and has no relevance to our plan. "Why does it matter?"

"It matters because Molay doesn't need to be present to keep the wards around the place up. As long as this is his anchor, whatever spell he's cast on your father will remain intact."

Sébastien snorts. "Spells and wards. What are you? A sorcerer?"

Le Chevalier d'Os laughs hoarsely. "I prefer ritualist." When he turns to me, his gaze is sombre again. "We can't just grab your father and be done with it. But the distraction still works in our favour. All we have to do is remove Molay's skeleton. Take it away, split it up, grind it up. And poof. That's how you kill a ghost."

Everything in me revolts against such a plan. My father and I didn't even dare touch the bones for fear of compromising them. If this ever gets out, I can never show my face in the historical community again. Of course, no one knows that Molay's skeleton even exists, but I know I'll never forget it. I think I'm going to be sick. "Is there really no other way?"

"What's wrong?" Sébastien asks with a deep frown.

Perhaps that I'm not a murderer? I'm not surprised that the Chevalier's plan involves the destruction of a ghost when he's supposedly murdered someone before. But to explain why it breaks my historian's heart to even consider it would take too much time. "He's still a person."

"No," says Sébastien with absolute conviction. "And the sooner you accept that, the easier your life will be."

I suppose that means he's not above a little ghost murder either. To him, Molay is a tool, or perhaps a weapon to be destroyed.

The Chevalier puts a hand on my shoulder, startling me. "I don't like it either, but if you can't convince Molay to let your father go, this is our only chance. And it will make the Boutique a lot safer. No more cataphiles suffering from inexplicable psychoses."

And here we are again. I'm paying too much attention to the dead and not enough to the living. I want to try and talk Molay out of this, but I'm not convinced I can reach him, and it would destroy the chance Victor will give us. There really is only one way. Anything else is misplaced idealism.

"Fine. Let's do it then."

Chapter 29

Our procession towards the Boutique of Psychosis is even more awkward now that the Chevalier has joined our team. He can't see Gaspar and Dix, but knowing him, he knows that at least one of them is there. Down here, though, he's the king, leading us on a completely different path to the Boutique, using a series of small corridors, hidden doors, and windows that I've never seen before. Even with my piece of the map, I wouldn't have found such a quick and direct route. We arrive near the Boutique almost an hour earlier than I expected.

Of course, this means we have to wait a little, as there's no way of telling Victor that we need him to summon Molay earlier. Sébastien and the Chevalier use the time to run through a number of different scenarios, some based on Molay not being there, contingency plans in case he returns early. Most of them involve the Chevalier performing a ritual while Sébastien keeps the ghosts away with salt bullets.

They have it all figured out. In every single scenario, my role is reduced to getting to my father and leading him out, while the men take care of everything else. All except the last one.

"What if it doesn't work?" Sébastien asks. "If he never leaves to have a ghost chat. He might not be interested, or Hugo himself might lose interest. He could forget the time. Or what if he warns Molay, and when we burst in, Molay is ready for us?"

Even though he hasn't spoken to me, I reply, "That won't happen. Victor is reliable."

"No ghost is reliable," says Sébastien with utter conviction.

"No ghost?" I look at Dix, who looks bored by all this strategising.

Sébastien follows my gaze. "Except for a whisper ghost. But Victor is not one of them. And neither is your friend." There's a hint of irritation in his voice when he mentions Gaspar. "You'll have to find your own whisper ghost to be of any use in the field."

The Chevalier leans back, watching us both without trying to intervene.

I swallow. I haven't told Sébastien that I've already found Petit Alix. To be honest, I don't think the little girl would have a chance of doing what Victor is. Besides, I'd never leave her alone with a creep like Molay, so I don't quite understand Sébastien's obsession with whisper ghosts.

"Well, I trust Victor. He's a man of his word. You may not believe in ghosts, but I do."

I can't be entirely sure, but I think I hear Sébastien muttering, "Which is why we're in this situation in the first place."

My annoyance with him grows. I started out liking him, but his attitude towards ghosts is downright grating. I expected more from someone whose whole job is to work with ghosts.

Without looking at me, Sébastien tells the Chevalier. "If he's in there, Alix will have to step in and do Hugo's job. Distract Molay long enough for us to do what's necessary."

"Perfect." Unlike Sébastien, the Chevalier nods at me in encouragement. "You've got this."

As much as it scares me to face Molay again after last night's meltdown, I feel equipped enough to do this little thing. The Grand Master knows I'll be back to negotiate for my father, whether I succeed or not.

"Very well." Sébastien rises from the ground. "Dix and I will see if the coast is clear. I'll send Dix when it's safe to follow."

I stay behind with the Chevalier and Gaspar, the latter massaging my shoulders and whispering in my ear, "Ignore that show-off. In my opinion, you're better than both of them."

To my utter horror, the Chevalier also leans in, keeping his voice low, "Don't tell Roubert when you find your whisper ghost."

Surprised, I stare at him. "Why not?"

"There's only one reason he's so interested in finding it: GoPol's main activity." When I frown, he glances down the dark tunnel, apparently fearing Dix's untimely return. "Have you ever wondered why there aren't more ghost whisperers?"

I hold my breath, dreading the answer.

"It's because GoPol rounds them up, takes them in, and eliminates them. The moment your whisper ghost ceases to exist," the Chevalier taps me on the forehead with his index finger, "your talent will also cease to exist. The moment you give your ghost to Roubert, he'll take your talent away from you."

CHAPTER 30

All hell breaks loose. Suddenly, ghosts appear around us and rush towards the column. Sébastien leaps into action, quickly firing shots of salt to keep the ghosts away. Dix mirrors him on the other side. When a ghost comes straight at me, Gaspar screams and throws himself at the other ghost. They both fall to the ground, but the attacker quickly wipes Gaspar off and for the first time I see Gaspar shimmering and flowing as you'd expect from a ghost. Unlike the ghosts in the Boutique, he's not at all tangible.

The same can't be said of Dix, who seems to rejoice every time his knee or the back of his hand connects with another ghost and sends them sprawling. His eyes glisten: I can even hear him laughing.

"Alix, I need you." The Chevalier was repeating his chant, but now he's beckoning me closer. "Here." He takes my hand and places it on Molay's skull above my father's drooping head. "Do you feel his spirit residue? I need you to pull it in here." He slides a black crystal into my other hand.

"What?"

"I can't do it with spells alone. I need you to use your special powers to capture the ghost."

"Seize him?" That doesn't sound right.

The Chevalier slaps his hand on mine. "Do it!"

The frenzy of the battle around me doesn't help my heightened anxiety. I try to tune it out, but it's hard with gunfire so close, even if it's just salt. It's only when the Chevalier starts his monotonous chant again that my mind manages to focus on the feeling beneath my fingers.

At first, it's nothing but bone. I push away the intruding thoughts about the sacrilege of touching an ancient skeleton without proper safeguards. I can't think like a historian here. That side of me won't help at all.

Instead, I close my eyes and concentrate on my skills. What is the Chevalier aiming at? What am I trying to feel here? What is there to grasp?

There! I can't quite explain it, but there's a kind of spark, something in the bones. A kind of presence.

I open my eyes and scream. The skeleton before me has come to life, and I'm looking straight into Molay's burning green eyes, my hand flat between them, fingers spread across his forehead.

"Don't…" the Chevalier says, but I stumble away, clutching my hand as if it were burned.

I bump into Gaspar, who's instantly at my side, while the Grand Master, dressed in his Templar robes, walks past my father, his frame towering over us. "You."

Speak, Alix. Distract him. I open my mouth, not knowing what to say to explain the chaos that has broken out in the Boutique. Just as a word floats to the top, my mouth inexplicably fills with water. A weight pulls me down and I gasp for air.

Help, I want to say, but all I can do is stutter. The waves break over me, throwing me to the ground.

It doesn't matter that it makes no sense at all, or that I can feel the hardness of the dry stone beneath me. In my mind I'm drowning anyway.

CHAPTER 31

I have to get to the surface to breathe! That's all I can think about, but I'm already there. Or rather, there is no surface. Darkness is waiting for me in every direction. I kick and wriggle, desperate for air. My lungs spasm, burning with the need for air denied them.

"Breathe, Alix! Breathe!" Gaspar shouts at me. His hands are wrapped around my jacket, trying to shake me out of it. "Breathe, damn it!"

He presses his mouth against mine, but he's already dead. There's no air to fill my lungs.

"Out of my way, ghost." Molay kicks him with his steel-toed boots, knocking Gaspar to the side and leaving me exposed. "You didn't hold up your end of the bargain, little girl."

A small part of my brain knows that I should be able to breathe perfectly well. There is no way I can drown here on dry land. I try my best, but as soon as I open my mouth, the feeling of water filling it washes all sense away. The lack of oxygen makes my vision blurry. All I can see is the glint of metal. Too late, I realise that Molay is bringing his big sword down on me.

He's going to kill me. He's going to—"Gaspar!"

The blade does not hit me. At the last second, Gaspar throws himself in front of me. At first the sword passes through his body like butter, but then it stops in his chest, as if he has suddenly come back to life—and been killed again, right in front of me.

A rush of air fills my lungs as the scream torn from my throat overwhelms the barrier of my mind. While I welcome the sudden clarity of my thoughts, the sight of Gaspar impaled on the sword is just as horrifying as the assault on my mind earlier.

He can't die again. He can't die again, I keep telling myself, but his body feels heavy in my arms as he slips from the sword, and blood that shouldn't be there quickly coats my hands. I try to keep the wound still, but he's practically been cut in half. "Stay with me!" I cry.

Gaspar gasps for air, blood bubbling from his lips. "Run. You have to get away." He grimaces in pain. "Don't mind me."

"So dramatic!" Dix jumps into the gap left by Gaspar and shoots Molay in the face. "Nice work hardening up in time though, lover boy." His flippant attitude takes an instant dive when he notices that the Grand Master has barely reacted to his injury and is already raising his sword again.

"What's wrong with you?" Dix shouts in disgust.

Molay taunts him. "You're in my realm, peasant, your guns won't work on me."

Of course they won't. In the Grand Master's lifetime, gunpowder hadn't even made its way down the Silk Road. He missed the great revolution by a few hundred years, and while a gun would always win a sword fight, it dawns on me that the rules of ghosts are different. It seems that Molay has spent very little time with the modern living, so he has no real idea what a weapon would do to him. Or perhaps it doesn't matter how much time he spends on Earth, his mind remains a reflection of 1314.

Swords may have gone out of fashion for a while, but modern people have no trouble imagining what they would be like. Gaspar fights his wound because he knows he'd be finished if this had happened in his lifetime. That's what Dix meant when he said to stop being so dramatic. He's already dead; the wound is as much an illusion as me drowning on dry land.

Someone grabs me from behind and pulls me to my feet. Gaspar slips from my grip. His head hits the ground, and he gasps for breath. But the blood is fading and there's no sticky residue on my hands.

"Help the Chevalier and then get out of here," Sébastien shouts at me. As soon as he's pushed me away, he raises his own gun. "Salt incoming!"

Dix ducks immediately. Sébastien fires a shot into Molay's chest. Unlike Dix's mirror weapon, this is the real thing. The bullet explodes on impact, tearing through the white coat and chest armour, dissolving them.

Sébastien reloads his gun with another bullet, not waiting for Molay to recover. His finger wraps around the trigger, but before he can aim again, three more ghosts jump at him. In an instant, Dix appears at Sébastien's back, taking the blows and guarding his whisperer. The two of them move in perfect unison, Dix's reactions perfectly complementing Sébastien's actions.

I'm completely mesmerised until suddenly Sébastien falters. He raises his shoulders as if startled by an invisible force. I don't know what he sees or hears, but suddenly he's lying flat on the floor, his eyes wide open. Shadows wrap around his arms and legs, pinning him to the ground as effectively as my father is pinned to the column. Within seconds, he's completely incapacitated.

"Shit!" Dix takes one look at Sébastien and almost falls apart. "Damn it, Séb! Snap out of it!"

He must be caught up in one of the Boutique's psychoses. Just like I was before. Sébastien's eyes are wide open. He's jerking his limbs, trying to free himself, grunting with the effort. When I turn around, the Chevalier is also on the floor, his head buried between his knees, whispering endlessly. Meanwhile, Dix is struggling to keep the ghosts away from him and Sébastien.

Jacques de Molay turns towards me, sword raised, eyes blazing. Behind him, Gaspar pushes himself to his knees before jumping onto Molay's back, only to be shaken off with a simple roll of his shoulder. I flinch as Gaspar slams to the ground, his ghostly wound reopening.

None of us stand a chance against this battle-hardened knight. His fighting skills and commanding aura have the entire room stacked against us. We are no match for him, least of all me. But I know some people who are.

"Alexandre de Beauharnais, I need you." I don't know if I'm saying it out loud or just thinking it hard, but if my gut feeling is correct, then I have the ability to summon ghosts, and a revolutionary general in my corner is exactly what we need.

The general flashes into existence right next to me. There's a moment of confusion, but then his life's training and instincts kick in almost instantly. His weapon appears a second later, the curved saber favoured by senior officers and nobles right up to the Napoleonic Wars. He deflects the blow and immediately counters with one of his own. Only then does he stop and look at me. "Alix?"

"Help me, please!"

His dark eyes narrow. "Of course."

"You would side with the living?" Molay thunders, turning to his new enemy.

"Give it a rest. They're the future. We're the past." And with that, Alexandre attacks Molay again, pulling him away from me.

Perfect. My plan is working. Time to call in a few favours.

It turns out my deliberate summoning leaves the ghosts little choice but to answer my call. I add a handful of decorated military officers from Alexandre's time whom I've met at the Panthéon. They may not have been ready to let anyone into their sanctuary, but they form a defensive circle around me without a moment's hesitation as they fend off the other ghosts.

I have no idea how long their memories will last in the Boutique, so I whirl around and attack the column with renewed vigour. The Chevalier is of little help, incapacitated by a tailor-made psychosis. I walk past him to relight two of the candles that have been extinguished, and lay my hand on Molay's skeleton, reviving my crusty Latin to repeat the words the Chevalier said before. And they said that Latin was a dead language.

Jacques de Molay must sense what I'm doing because I suddenly feel an overwhelming sense of dread. Shadows are wrapping around my body, crawling under my skin. I try to ignore them, telling myself it's just one of the Boutique's many tricks.

Weaken the seal.

The shadows crawl up my neck, strangely caressing my cheek.

Weaken the seal.

It flows into my nostrils and fills my mouth. I gasp for air, coming up short again.

Weaken the seal.

It's the same feeling as drowning, only this time I'm determined to resist. I need Molay's core. Need—

Something cracks like thunder. I draw in a breath as a sharp pain erupts in my chest. It feels as if a rib has broken. If I continue on this course, more will break. I will break.

I shake my head in defiance. "No. You break!"

Break the seal.

Thunder shakes the room as the chains around the column explode outwards. The force throws me backwards onto my back. My father falls to his knees, half landing on my legs, and the sensation of the shadows drowning me disappears.

It worked. *It worked!*

"Big mistake, little girl." Somehow the Grand Master appears right on top of me, his sword raised directly above my chest. *He can't hurt me. He can't—*

The tip dissolves before my eyes until the whole sword disintegrates, followed by Jacques de Molay. With a horrified look, he vanishes into thin air.

"There we go," the Chevalier's calm voice can be heard not far from me.

I look up to see him stuffing the charred skull into his pack. As he pulls on the string, the shadows recede, and the noise dies away. Every trace of the last Grand Master of the Knights Templar has been erased.

His followers have fallen to their knees, their arms raised in defeat. The spirits I have summoned raise their weapons. Jean Lannes shouts, "I haven't had this much fun since Montebello!" He turns to me. "You should have called us sooner. We would have gladly taken care of that cretin."

"I'll remember that for next time." What am I saying? Next time? There won't be a next time. Not if I can help it.

"Who are all these people?" Sébastien is on his feet again. He looks around cautiously, his breath still ragged.

I carefully pull myself out from under my father's weight and up into a sitting position before cradling him in my arms. After checking that he's breathing, I answer Sébastien's question: "Well, this is Jean Lannes de Montebello, also known as the Prince of Siewirz. He fought in the revolutionary wars and under Napoleon, and was one of his most daring and talented generals. This is Michel Ordener, one of Napoleon's Imperial Guards." Napoleon put a lot of his pals in the Panthéon when he was in charge.

"While here we have Alexandre de Beauharnais, who fought in the Great Revolution but fell to the guillotine a few days before the fall of the Reign of Terror. Sorry, I shouldn't have mentioned that," I apologise to Alexandre.

"That's what people remember. That and my ex-wife," he adds with a grin, before glancing at Napoleon's generals. Had he lived a little longer, he would have been one of them, but history had other plans. "Do you want me to keep this quiet from your grand-mother?"

"Yes, please." As encouraging as she is of my non-relationship with Gaspar, she'll pull out the concerned grandmother card if she finds out what happened here.

Sébastien looks at me as if I've gone mad. "Your grandmother. Who's she? Napoleon's mistress?"

I can't help laughing, the sound eerie in the silent Boutique. "She wasn't that old. My grandmother is just an ordinary ghost, no one special."

"Wrong. Estelle is a very special woman," Alexandre protests, defending his crush.

Sébastien stares in complete bewilderment. "This is insane."

Dix throws his arm around Sébastien and grins wildly at me. "Nah, it's awesome! Alix is pretty special herself. Can we keep her?"

The exhilaration of having survived this battle fades as I re-member what the Chevalier warned me about. I can't tell if Dix's comment was just a casual joke or if it was an allusion to GoPol's mission, but if the Chevalier is right, there's no way they're going to keep me around.

Speaking of the Chevalier, he seems to have deconstructed the entire skeleton and divided the bones into several black sacks. I suppress my initial protest at witnessing this destruction of history. It almost hurts me physically, but rehabilitating Jacques de Molay is out of the question now. Remembering him is simply too dangerous.

Slowly, the ghosts take their leave. With a salute to Alexandre, the Panthéon ghosts disappear. Alexandre lingers a moment longer to examine my father, whose eyes are still moving rapidly behind his eyelids. "It's Estelle's boy. Are you sure I should keep it a secret from her?"

Fear pierces my heart. "Won't he be alright?"

Alexandre shrugs. "I don't know. I've never seen anything like it."

Just then, my father groans. His eyelids flutter and a moment later his eyes open. "Alix?"

Tears stream down my face as I smile at him. "Welcome back, Papa."

I help him to sit up and he does so with a groan. "What happened? Who are these guys?"

Sébastien takes the initiative and kneels down in front of him. "Sébastien Roubert, I'm a policeman. Alix called me to help. And I think your daughter Hélène is going to marry my cousin?"

Still confused, Papa shakes his hand. "Nice to meet you, what was it? Sébastien."

"Do you remember anything from... before?"

I watch my father anxiously as he tries to remember what happened before. "It's all a bit fuzzy. Did I fall? My head hurts like

I did. And I..." He shudders. His eyes turn inward, as if there's something to see in his mind. "Never mind."

Sébastien and I exchange worried glances. It's not yet clear whether my father remembers anything of his ordeal at the hands of Jacques de Molay. "Let's see if you can stand." Sébastien offers him both his hands and pulls my father up. "How's that?"

By now the Chevalier has finished packing up Molay's bones and slips over to my side. "I have no idea what you were doing in here, but I want to know all about it. You know where to find me when you're ready to leave GoPol behind."

"Wait," I whisper, not wanting him to get away so easily. "What about Molay? Why are you taking the bones?"

He lowers his voice, not wanting to alert my father. "I'm spreading them out. That's the whole trick. You understand why, don't you?"

It takes me a moment, but then I understand. By scattering Molay's bones, he'll destroy his sense of self, and since there's no strong base anywhere else to remember him, he'll fade into obscurity. Even if he lingers, he'll never be whole, just like the ghosts in the public part of the catacombs.

As soon as the Chevalier sees that I understand, he pats me on the shoulder and nods. "Remember what I said." Then he leaves.

Sébastien notices but doesn't say anything. "Let's pack up and go home."

I hurry to my father's side and offer him my support. "Are you alright?"

"Yes, yes, I will be. Sorry I scared you, kid." He plants a kiss on my hair. "You did well. The policeman praised your quick thinking."

I look at Sébastien and silently thank him for handling the situation so well. He shrugs, but his eyes tell me we'll have a lot to talk about. But not in front of my father.

As we leave the Boutique of Psychosis behind us, Dix steadies Gaspar. He looks much better than before, but he still seems to be struggling a bit. "Don't worry, History Girl. He'll be back to normal in no time."

With my father here, I can only smile at them. I'm glad that Dix has dropped the hostility and is helping Gaspar out while I'm otherwise occupied. It seems Gaspar has earned the other man's respect by saving my life. He's definitely earned mine.

CHAPTER 32

Sébastien accompanied us to the hospital to have my father examined, but they couldn't find anything wrong with him and just suggested he rest. But while we were waiting, Sébastien told me to find my ghost. "The sooner you do, the safer you'll be."

After the fight in the Boutique of Psychosis, I can't trust him in good conscience. There's no way Petit Alix would have contributed anything to the fight. It would have been horrible for her to be there and see all that.

It sucks because I want to know more about the whisper ghosts and Sébastien is the only one who could tell me about them. But if he says I'll be safer, it must be because he really wants to take away my whisper powers, and that's out of the question for many reasons.

Most importantly, this little girl deserves a family to love her after the twenty years she's spent in a wet hell. And I just so happen to know the perfect couple.

"You want us to have her?" Abelard asks, his voice hoarse with emotion.

"If you'll have her." At the moment the little girl is settled in Gaspar's arms, but in our current situation this can only be a temporary measure. "I need you to keep her safe. Can you do that?"

"Who's after her?" Héloïse asks, picking up on the underlying threat.

I look over my shoulder, unable to shake the paranoia I've been carrying since the Boutique. "Hopefully nobody, but there's a chance someone will. They'll end her."

"End this sweet little baby?" Abelard is outraged. He holds out his arms. "Give her to me."

I watch as Gaspar gently passes the toddler ghost on. "These two are going to be your new maman and papa. Isn't that exciting?"

Petit Alix seems a little sceptical, but as soon as Abelard wraps her in his arms, she lays her head on his shoulder, making me wonder if she trusts ghosts by nature. "Will you go away?" she asks Abelard, breaking my heart.

"Never." From the tone of his voice, he's already decided to protect this little girl with his entire existence. "Come, I'll show you where we live." He took her to the top of the hill to show her Père Lachaise below.

Héloïse takes my hands and squeezes them. "I don't know how to thank you, except to thank you for healing his pain."

It's so heartfelt, I don't know what to say. "You're really doing me a favour." I can't bear to lose my ability. For once, I don't want to lose these connections I've made with the ghosts. I'm still a little angry with some of the Panthéon ghosts, but they're mostly my friends. And I want to help other ghosts—so long as they don't turn out to be devil-worshipping psychos. But most of all, I don't want to lose Gaspar.

Gaspar takes my hand and lifts it to his mouth, planting a soft kiss on my knuckles. "Let's go home."

We stroll down the hill, hand in hand. As we pass my grandmother, she and Beatrice have Alexandre over again. The three of them seem to be enjoying themselves and Gaspar and I decide not to interrupt their little get-together.

"Why didn't you choose your grandmother and her beau?" Gaspar asks. "She's known you since you were a little kid, and he's a damn good fighter."

"Because they'd be too obvious. Sébastien already knows too much about them."

"You really think he'd do that to you?"

I shrug. "I can't be one hundred percent sure, but it's not something I'm willing to risk. He's a stickler for rules, and if the Chevalier is right, that's the number one rule in GoPol."

"Hmm. I suppose you won't be joining the police any time soon?" Gaspar jokes.

I laugh at him. "No, no, that's out of the question. Besides, I'm not cut out for it."

"You saved everyone's ass down there by calling in all those highly decorated military officers. And then some."

When he puts it like that, I didn't do too badly. Still, the thought of a repeat keeps me awake at night. Sébastien, the Chevalier, and I barely made it out of the Boutique alive, and Dix and Gaspar were completely overpowered. No, the days of fighting ghosts in the catacombs are over.

Back home, Gaspar slips into my room. At this time of night, everyone else is asleep, so no one minds if I talk quietly to myself. We sit on the bed, Malou between us, me leaning against him, his arm around my shoulder.

"I've worked out what I'm going to do now that I'm dead," Gaspar says, sounding determined.

"Yeah? And what's that?" I have an idea, but I'm curious to see if I'm right.

"It's funny. When I was alive and studying, I had no idea what I wanted out of life. There were some paths that seemed more tempting than others, but I thought I had all the time in the world. Now I have all the time in the world, but I couldn't see any options. Until we took on the Panthéon."

I grimace. I haven't yet made up my mind whether I really want to quit as planned. The military officers came through when I called them, and Victor did his part as well, but a lot of hurt has been thrown in both directions. "Don't tell me you want to force them to open their ivory tower?"

"No, I've just realised that there's an imbalance of power that leaves a lot of ordinary ghosts to fend for themselves. Jacques de Molay may have gone way off course, but I like the general idea of Nexus. Of creating a community. The afterlife is so scattered. I want to bring people together. Not by creating rules and hierarchies, but by identifying their common needs..." He laughs nervously. "Look, I'm no expert—I barely had two years of social studies. But I want to try."

He glances nervously at me and catches me smiling at him. "I love it," I whisper. "It's a wonderful idea."

"You love it?" He sounds so relieved.

"Yes." I shuffle closer, making sure Malou doesn't get squashed. My heart is beating so loudly I'm sure he can hear it. "If anything, it makes me love you even more."

Surprised, Gaspar raises his eyebrows. "You... what are you saying?"

"I've tried to do the sensible thing, the socially acceptable thing, but I can't fight it any longer." Not after seeing Gaspar doting on Petit Alix, or seeing him take the blow that was meant for me, or saving me from the cold floods of the Seine. "I love you, ghost or not."

Gaspar swallows. "But..."

I slip my hand around his neck and look deep into his eyes. "You heard Abelard. The feelings won't go away. I know it's unconventional, but I don't want to run away from you anymore."

His arm moves to my lower back. He pulls me closer until our chests and foreheads touch. "Good, because I'm not going to let you get away that easily."

Heat flushes my cheeks and my lips curve into a broad smile. Gaspar leans in and kisses me softly. It's the first time we've been intimate since that night at the Panthéon, and it makes me wonder what the hell I've been worrying about. It feels good. Like coming home. Like we always belonged together. Being apart hurts too much, but for all its wrongness, this feels right.

A knock startles us. The door opens and my papa looks in. "Alix, I'm-I'm sorry. I didn't know you had company. Never mind. Carry on." With a fleeting smile, he ducks out again.

"Alix?" Gaspar's voice is muffled as I stare at the door with my mouth hanging open.

Papa has seen us. He's *seen* Gaspar.

What happened to him in the Boutique of Psychosis?

Thank you for reading Ghosts of the Catacombs. The adventure will continue in Ghosts of the Resistance (Parisian Ghosts 2). <u>Order here</u>

Want to read more? If you liked Alix, Gaby, and Malou and want to read more of their adventures, sign up to my Story Seeker Newsletter to get a free Parisian Ghosts prequel that takes place two years prior to the events of Ghosts of the Catacombs, featuring Josephine Baker. Plus, you'll alway stay on top of spooky news from Janna Ruth (and Malou). <u>Sign up</u>

Please review! Authors depend on reviews to get the word out about their books. If you enjoyed Ghosts of the Catacombs, consider reviewing it on your favourite retailer, review site or your personal blog.

Want some fun? If you want to chat with me and other readers about my various books, join my Facebook group. We will read together, discuss details, and have some fun with games and give-aways. <u>Join the Story Seekers</u>

278

Afterword

What a rollercoaster ride! Alix was really put through her paces in this book. It might have been a bit slower as a result, but hopefully it didn't pull any emotional punches.

Speaking of emotional punches, her journey is far from over. Will GoPol really try to take away her powers? Will this send her into the arms of the Chevalier? And how will her family dynamics change now that her father is also a ghost whisperer? Book 3 will have the answers to these questions and many more, so don't miss out.

I hope you enjoyed this foray into the City of Lights and the dark and mysterious city below. We will continue to explore Paris and all its famous places. We will meet more famous people, taste more French food, and uncover more secrets.

Thanks to my Story Seekers who voted for *Parisian Ghosts* to be my next series. Whether you follow me on Facebook or subscribe to my newsletter, you're the reason I tell these stories.

For Parisian Ghosts I tried something new and did a crowdfunding campaign. Twenty-two amazing people pledged their support and helped me develop the series. I hope you're pleased with the final result. Thank you for believing in me, Alix and Malou.

A special thank you goes to Chris Rowan, my French advisor and dear author friend, as well as my main beta reader for the series. Thank you for answering all my weirdly specific and non-specific questions and for supporting the story before it was even a thing. I am inspired by your own success. You're doing great, man. Long may it continue.

Malou would like to thank Laura Greenwood for enabling hedgehogs to take over the book world and for supporting her worm dominance with appropriate games, fun, and tummy rubs. I promise Malou got every belly rub she deserved for collecting pre-orders, even if not all of them made it onto the page.

A big thank you to all the FAKAs, some of whom supported me as beta readers, by pledging their support, or just by cheering me on. You know who you are. Keep kicking ass. The same goes for all the beta readers who aren't writers, but amazing, detail-oriented readers. Love you all!

Jackie, I don't know what I'd do without our often-daily Zoom sessions. Thank you for holding me accountable, listening to all my worries, and helping to shape *Parisian Ghosts* into what it is today. I'm so glad I met you!

And, of course, thank you to all the wonderful, amazing readers and followers on Facebook, TikTok, my newsletter and wherever else I've picked you up. You have made the build-up to this series so much fun. Thank you for joining the Malou hype and making her the best pre-order hedgehog ever ;) See you all back for *Ghosts of the Resistance!*

Love,

Janna

THE ADVENTURE CONTINUES...

I've given the ghosts everything. Now they're coming for my powers.

All my life, I've talked to ghosts, helped them fulfil their last wishes, and made friends with them. I thought I had a good grip on the afterlife. Boy, was I wrong. There are things afoot in the beyond that make my nightmares have nightmares.

After wiping a powerful ghost from existence, his followers are out for blood. My blood. As if that weren't bad enough, my allies cannot be trusted. Down in the catacombs, the Knight of Bones is seizing control of powerful ghost dwellings for reasons that make my stomach turn. Meanwhile my acquaintances at GoPol have branded me an unnecessary risk to be exterminated.

My only chance of escaping with my life and my powers intact is to join the Resistance. If I can't convince the rogue ghosts and whisperers hiding in the old bunkers of Paris to help me, I'll lose everything. My ghost friends, my ability, but most importantly, the love of my life.

Urban Fantasy with a French twist. If you like cave-crawling adventures, hopeless romantics, and ghosts, you'll enjoy Ghosts of the Resistance, the third book of the Parisian Ghosts series. Travel to Paris today to embark on your catacomb adventure.

Read here

Also by Janna Ruth

To see the Erlking's face is to see your own death

Nature spirits have ravaged the world with natural disasters for millennia. They're dangerous, unpredictable, and largely invisible. After eight years living on the streets, Rika is one of the few people in the world that can see them. Most of the time, she keeps a fragile peace with them, but when the Erlking, a powerful storm sprite, attacks Berlin, Rika is drawn into the war against nature.

She joins the spirit seekers, a group of elite soldiers trained to defend Berlin and other cities around the world from nature's wrath. Currently bereaved of their acting commander, the spirit seekers look to Rika to be their eyes, but when Rika befriends a young sylph, she isn't even sure she wants to fight spirits. Her hand is forced when she comes face to face with the Erlking though, an incident that can have only one possible outcome: her death.

Join the Spirit Seekers in their first, stormy adventure and start your European journey today!

<u>Read here</u>

ALSO BY JANNA RUTH

Magic, Demons and High School Drama

All Lucille ever wanted was a perfectly normal high school experience, but her town doesn't do normal. Not when a few Latin words set her hand on fire, the entire town gets possessed by evil spirits, and the cute guy she's got her eyes on brings a freaking sword to the battle.

Now Lucille has to make a decision: return to her cushy, and safe, life-style at the boarding school, or join her friends and face the monsters that hunt her and the magic that resides inside of her.

A Drop of Magic is the first book of this action-packed, ensemble-led YA fantasy series with the wit of Buffy, the magic of Charmed, and all the drama of the Vampire Diaries. Join Lucille and her friends on their monster hunt!

<u>Read here</u>

READ FOR FREE

When an undead movie star asks you for a small favour, you know you're gonna be in deep trouble.

Seeing ghosts is just something I've learnt to live with. They're everywhere I go, especially since I chose to study history at the Sorbonne, one of the oldest universities in the world. While on a class trip to the Pantheon, where France's great men—and women!—reside, I get introduced to the fabulous Josephine Baker! One of her war medals has gone missing, and she wants me to find its whereabouts.

Who could say no to a flapper girl turned movie star turned war hero? Little do I know agreeing to do so will send me on a wild-goose chase across the country with a ghostly pet cheetah, hidden walkways, and a murder attempt.

Follow Alix on her first big ghost adventure two years prior to the events of Parisian Ghosts.

<u>Sign up</u> to my Story Seeker mailing list and grab the prequel for free

About Janna Ruth

Once upon a time, Janna Ruth studied the plate boundaries of this world. Now, she's creating her own worlds. Born in Berlin, Germany, Janna lives in Wellington, New Zealand, writing both English and German books.

Janna's writing career kicked off when she won a writing competition for German publisher Ueberreuter. Her first self-published novel "Im Bann der zertanzten Schuhe" (Melody of Curse, coming in June 2022) went on to win the 2018 SERAPH for "Best Independent Title". She debuted in English with her witchy novella "Witching with Dolphins" in 2020 and has since published urban fantasy, YA sci-fi, and contemporary coming-of-age novels and series.

When Janna isn't writing, she has a plethora of hobbies, such as aerial acrobatics, cake decorating, drawing, reading, and anything crafty you can throw her way.

Find out more about Janna and her books here:

- **Website:** www.janna-ruth.com

- **BookBub:** www.bookbub.com/authors/janna-ruth

- **Facebook:** www.facebook.com/authorjannaruth

- **Facebook Reader Group:** www.facebook.com/groups/471802574687199

- **Goodreads:** www.goodreads.com/author/show/16513923.Janna_Ruth

- **Twitter:** www.twitter.com/jannaRuthAuthor

- **Instagram:** www.instagram.com/janna_ruth

- **TikTok:** www.tiktok.com/@jannaruthwrites

- **Pinterest:** www.pinterest.com/jannaruthwrites